D

Everyone here at JOVE and all our authors are simply thrilled by the enthusiastic reception you've given to SECOND CHANCE AT LOVE!

We have lots of marvelous love stories coming up for the fall and winter by both seasoned pros and the brand-new talent we're very proud to be able to present. Our goal is to give you wholesome, heart-warming, yet exciting romances that are a pleasure to read. So, of course, your opinion about how well we're doing is very important to us, and we love to have your reactions to our SECOND CHANCE AT LOVE novels. Do let us hear from *you*!

Again, thanks for so warmly welcoming SECOND CHANCE AT LOVE. Your response has encouraged and inspired us.

With every good wish,

Carolyn Nichols

Carolyn Nichols
SECOND CHANCE AT L
Jove Publications, Inc.
200 Madison Avenue
New York, New Yor

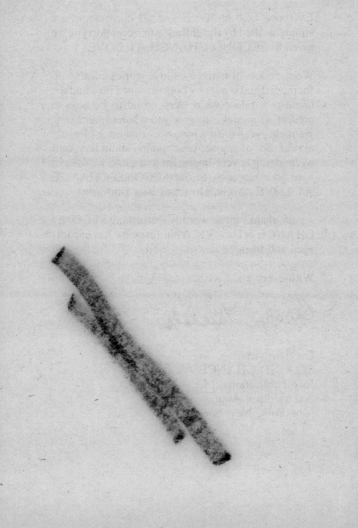

"We'd better go back," he murmured huskily against her skin...

She made an inarticulate sound of protest. They stood side by side, gazing out at the obsidian ocean, his arm around her waist.

She leaned her head against his shoulder, closing her eyes. It seemed forever before she felt his mouth, cool and firm as she knew it would be, lacking any haste or urgency as he took little exploratory tastes of her lips.

She pulled his head downward in an involuntary effort to satisfy the restless hunger he aroused. Her gesture of impatience, her imploring moan, snapped his restraint, and his mouth moved on hers, fiercely devouring. And she yielded to this man she could no longer deny...

MEETING WITH THE PAST
CAROLINE HALTER

A JOVE BOOK

Requests for permission to make copies of any part of the work should be mailed to: Permissions, "Second Chance at Love," Jove Publications, Inc., 200 Madison Avenue, New York, NY 10016

First Jove edition published September 1981

"Second Chance at Love" and the butterfly emblem are trademarks belonging to Jove Publications, Inc.

Printed in the United States of America

Jove books are published by Jove Publications, Inc., 200 Madison Avenue, New York, NY 10016

Chapter One

"HOW DOES IT feel to be a free woman, Alex?"

"It feels great, Jinx," Alex replied swiftly, mustering a smile that felt too stiff on her features to convince anyone as perceptive as Jinx. Alex didn't feel particularly good about anything right now, as much as she had looked forward to this moment for months. Up to now she had tried to rationalize and convince herself that the breakup of her marriage wasn't entirely *her* fault. If that was true, why did she have this heavy sense of inadequacy and failure?

"You don't know how grateful I am to you," she began, only to be interrupted by an expletive no dyed-in-the-wool lady would let past her lips.

"Save all that gratitude, Alex. We fat cat lawyers just do our job for the big fees."

The cynical words and hard tone didn't fool Alex for

1

one second. She saw the expression of concern in the sharp blue eyes regarding her closely. But for the moment she abandoned the effort to verbalize the debt she felt to this woman who had been far more than a lawyer to her during the difficult months between her separation and divorce decree, which became final today. Martha Jenson, called Jinx because of some now long forgotten mishaps early in her legal career, was leaning back in her swivel chair with hands clasped behind her head and high-heel-clad feet resting on the desk top in a most unlawyerlike manner. Alex smiled warmly. Jinx had battled for her with all the ferocity of a mother wolf protecting her young from the dangers of the wild, in this instance represented by Courtney and his lawyers, who attempted time after time to bully her into terms totally to his advantage.

Jinx had also listened, sympathized, scolded, and at times done her own share of bullying, all for Alex's best interests. Alex had been far too vulnerable and confused to think and act for herself, and except for one major decision, upon which she remained firm in spite of all the efforts Jinx made to sway her, she had given herself over totally into her lawyer's hands.

"Have you thought about what you're going to do now?" Jinx frowned at Alex's slight shrug and vague expression. "I know you don't have any immediate worries, Alex, but keep in mind that you *are* going to have to support yourself eventually. The marriage settlement is a good cushion between you and the bill collectors, but with inflation it won't last indefinitely."

"I know, I know, Jinx." Alex held up one hand as if to ward off the censure in the other woman's voice and manner. "You still think I should have asked for alimony. Maybe you were right. In fact, you probably *were*. But you know my reasons." Her low voice pleaded to be understood. Her fine hazel eyes were clouded with unhappiness; her full mouth drooped.

"Right now you don't need sympathy. You need

someone to prod you into getting on with the business of living. You insisted you wanted a '*clean break*,'" Jinx continued, "but a divorce isn't quite the same as breaking a bone, Alex. One has to live during the recovery period. Not just pay the rent and utility bills, but afford some of the amenities that make life worthwhile. I don't have to remind you that you married right out of high school, and the past seven years as Mrs. Courtney Jameson haven't exactly prepared you to earn a decent living."

Alex struggled to hold back tears, despising herself for being such a spineless ninny when she wanted more than anything to be brave and optimistic—at the very least for Jinx's benefit. The attempt at a laugh came out as a choked sob. "Isn't it strange? I've looked forward to this day and tried to imagine what it would feel like to be... free. I never dreamed I would feel so rotten..." Her voice broke and she bit her quivering lip with teeth that were white and perfectly even, unable now to prevent the flow of tears down her face. "Jinx, tell me the truth. Do you think I was wrong to leave Courtney? Do you think—"

"*Stop it this minute, Alex!*" Jinx commanded, bringing her feet down to the floor and squaring her shoulders like a general. "This kind of thinking will get you nowhere. Have you forgotten so soon that your husband not only had one affair after another but didn't even bother to conceal the fact from you? Could you have lived with that kind of situation and kept your self-respect?"

"But it was partly my fault. He said..."

"I could murder Courtney Jameson for his unspeakable cruelty. He's undermined your confidence in yourself as a desirable woman by insisting he had affairs with other women because you're frigid." Jinx sighed. "Nothing I can say will convince you, Alex. God knows I've already tried. You're just going to have to find out for yourself that with the right man you're a perfectly normal woman in every way. You're just better looking than most, and that's going to cause you some problems."

There was a rueful look in Alex's hazel eyes. "It already has, hasn't it?"

Alex nodded. "*Everything* you warned me about has been true, Jinx. It's so degrading the way men assume I'm starved for sex just because I'm no longer living with Courtney. I was shocked, too, at some of the men who've called. I never dreamed..." She let her voice drift off, knowing from the worldy-wise expression on Jinx's face that she didn't have to explain how appalled she had been to receive blatantly open propositions from several men she had assumed were happily married family types. And then there were those well-intentioned friends who wanted to "fix her up" with one of their single male acquaintances.

"After a while people will leave you alone," Jinx assured her. "Meanwhile you may have to come right out and tell them to mind their own business."

The emotional storm in Alex was beginning to subside. The day a divorce was final was frequently very traumatic, she had heard time and again from Jinx. It was a day that brought on a siege of self-doubt and guilt. There was one last hurdle to go over, and the silence lengthened as she gathered courage to speak of the subject which brought deep pain.

"Maybe if I'd been able to have a child—"

"You don't really believe that," Jinx cut in sharply. "A child is no magic remedy for an ailing marriage. Look at the divorce statistics, if you won't believe me. And there's no reason to blame yourself because you and Courtney didn't have children. Didn't you tell me the doctors were unable to find anything wrong with you? And didn't Courtney outright refuse to even undergo an examination?" She stood up with the finality of a judge who has just pronounced sentence and rapped the gavel to adjourn the court. "Now what say we go to lunch? It's about time for some of that clean-break psychology I've heard so much about."

Alex felt an overwhelming relief to have the session

over. It had been grueling but necessary to expose to someone else the guilt feelings that were like cancerous growths undermining her optimism for the future. Somehow dragging them out into the open like this was therapeutic.

Over lunch, Jinx again brought up the subject of Alex's future. "What would you *really* like to do, I mean if you could do *anything* you wanted to?"

"I'd love to travel!" The answer just popped out without any consideration, surprising Alex more than Jinx, who looked immensely pleased with herself.

"Hmm, let's see. What are some jobs that might involve travel opportunities? What about an airline?"

"Oh, I'm probably too old to train for flight attendant," Alex protested, but her cheeks had twin spots of color and the hazel eyes were no longer clouded. They held green flecks of excitement. For the first time since she had decided she could no longer maintain the hypocrisy of her marriage, she felt a surge of hope for her future.

"A good friend of mine out in San Francisco works for a travel agency," Jinx offered thoughtfully. "She goes somewhere exotic at least twice a year. I'm quite sure she gets reduced rates on flights and hotel accommodations, and sometimes the agency picks up the whole tab when it's a package tour they offer."

Jinx dropped the subject soon after that. Alex was glad because she needed time to examine the new discovery she had made about herself—and to look at her prospects realistically. There was danger in building up hopes for the kind of job that might be impossible for her to land. When the two women parted with mutual promises to stay in touch, Alex felt confident for the first time that she would be able to cope with certain immediate problems and decisions. For one thing, she had been living at home with her parents, and as much as she appreciated their support through the ordeal of her separation and divorce proceedings, she had to get a place of her own soon. Up until now she hadn't mustered

the courage to contest their assumption that she would
continue living with them in the same house in which
she had grown up. They were wonderful, loving parents,
but she was a mature woman now, not a child, and she
needed to be on her own.

Engrossed in these thoughts about her immediate future, she braked for a red light in the center of the main
business district. She had grown up in this medium-size
town in northern Georgia, married here, and lived in one
of the affluent country club subdivisions during the seven
years of her marriage. Today during lunch when she had
blurted out her desire to travel, it had come as a revelation
just how limited her twenty-five years had been. Suddenly she felt stifled.

The light turned green, and she accelerated. Up ahead
on her right was Globe Travel Unlimited ... and there
was an empty parking space directly in front! An omen,
Alex thought. Nothing less than an omen! She flipped
on her turn signal and maneuvered her compact car into
the space.

Her stomach fluttered from nervousness as she stood
outside the plate-glass windows, studying travel posters
that urged people to discover foreign lands. The world
seemed large and full of infinite possibilities she couldn't
wait to explore now that she was free. *Free!* The realization hit her that nothing except her own timidity could
hold her back from doing *whatever* she wanted to do.
And she wanted to travel.

She pushed open the door and stood just inside a large
room, a little bewildered because there was so much to
attract the eye. Large travel posters on the wall and racks
of brochures broadcast the dozens of new places to go,
novel experiences to sample. It was quite overwhelming.

"Can I help you?"

Alex became aware of a young brunette woman sitting
behind one of the four desks in the room. The others
weren't occupied, reminding Alex that it was still lunchtime. Perhaps that knowledge gave her the courage she

needed, since there was a good chance the manager was out too.

"I'd like to speak to the manager," she announced, advancing to the center of the room.

"Who may I say would like to see him?" came the automatic response.

"Alex Jameson." Alex met the curiosity in the brown eyes and felt a twinge of compunction for using Courtney's name, which was well known in Stokely. Yet Jameson *was* still legally her name, even if she was no longer married to Courtney.

The young woman hesitated briefly, then rose and walked to a connecting door, which was ajar. Alex could hear her voice, then the deeper cadences of masculine voices. The manager was obviously busy, she realized with a blend of relief and disappointment. Would she have nerve enough to come back later? Right now she was functioning on the adrenaline that came from unfounded optimism, not on any sound confidence in her own capabilities.

The brunette returned, curiosity even stronger in the brown eyes. "Mr. Campbell will see you in one moment, Mrs. Jameson. Have a seat over here." She motioned to a chair beside one of the unoccupied desks.

Alex had just sat down when the manager appeared, a man in his mid-thirties with thinning blond hair and hearty blue eyes. "Brian Campbell," he said, offering her his hand and then sitting down behind the desk. She was mildly surprised, having assumed he would invite her into his office where they could talk in private. But then she remembered the other masculine voice and concluded that he had been interrupted in the middle of some business and didn't plan to take long with her. It was awkward to have to talk in front of the young woman, who had resumed her original seat and radiated curiosity.

To compensate for her nervousness, Alex spoke louder than was necessary. "I'd like to place a job application," she announced firmly, aware that Brian

Campbell was looking her over rather thoroughly. And she was aware, too, that he wasn't displeased with what he saw—a tall, slender young woman with tawny hair and startlingly beautiful hazel eyes. She didn't know that he was eyeing the expensive cut of her suit and wondering if she was one of *the* Jamesons in Stokely. It didn't add up.

"I see. You've had experience as a travel agent, Mrs. Jameson?"

"*Miss* Jameson as of today," she corrected and read the instant comprehension in his face. "And I don't have experience, but I *am* very interested in travel. I'm sure I could learn." Again her voice seemed to echo around the room. She could read the polite refusal in his face even before he said the first word.

"At the present time we really don't have—" The telephone in front of him buzzed insistently. He looked down in surprise at the lighted button and said politely, "Excuse me one moment, please. Yes?" he spoke into the receiver.

As he listened to the voice on the phone, his eyes widened and then narrowed as they flickered once again over Alex. "Will do," he injected at one point and then, after a level "You're the boss," hung up.

Alex summoned a brave smile, having had time during the telephone conversation to harden herself to the inevitable. Her smile froze in amazement at his next words.

"You're free to travel, Miss Jameson? No problems such as young children?"

"Why, yes—that is, no. I mean I *am* free to travel and I don't have any children at all," she murmured in some confusion.

"We may have something you'd be interested in. Let me take down some information about you, just in case." With those astounding words, he took up a pen that was lying on the desk and began to ask her questions, jotting the answers on a pad. The most she had expected was the opportunity to fill out a standard application form.

This personal interrogation by the manager was far more promising.

When he seemed satisfied, he stood up behind the desk and extended his hand again. "I'll let you know one way or the other in a day or two."

Alex left then, her head reeling. Could she really be so lucky to walk into a job that involved travel—just like that? It was too good to be true, too thrilling to believe.

By the next afternoon Alex was a bundle of frayed nerves, sitting around her parents' house waiting for the telephone to ring. She hadn't confided in anyone about her job interview, as if afraid that talking about the job would spoil her chances of getting it.

By lunchtime the following day, she had despaired of ever hearing from Brian Campbell. He probably had thought better of hiring someone so inexperienced, she reasoned despondently. Or maybe the job hadn't materialized after all. There was always the possibility that someone more qualified than she had come along, too. But he *had* promised to telephone "one way or the other," hadn't he?

In the midst of agonizing over all the reasons the manager of Globe Travel Unlimited had not called, she heard the telephone ring. "Hello," she said absent-mindedly into the receiver and then stammered foolishly as the identity of the caller finally sank in. "M—Mister Campbell, it's you! I didn't think—that is, when you didn't. . . . Why yes, of course. I can come in this afternoon. Two o'clock? That will be fine. Just fine!"

When she greeted him two hours later, it was with the knowledge that she looked her best—her hair, styled so it didn't quite reach her shoulders, gleamed from its recent shampoo, the color a rich honey brown. She had taken some pains with her make-up too, applying mascara to emphasize the length and thickness of eyelashes more than one woman acquaintance had cattily dismissed as false. A subtle touch of pale green eyeshadow brought out the flecks of the same color in her clear hazel eyes.

"You're looking even *more* lovely this afternoon, Alex. You don't mind if we dispense with the formalities right off? We operate on a first name basis around here."

Alex warmed to the admiration in his eyes, shaking her head to his question, which was in effect merely rhetorical. "Of course I don't mind, Mr. Campbell." Then realizing the contradiction of her reply, she laughed in genuine amusement at herself, the first time she had *really* laughed in a long, long time, she realized with sudden insight. The merriment at her own expense erased the tension she had felt since the telephone call. She sat down, this time in his office, relaxed and eager to hear what he had to say.

"What do you know about Globe Travel Unlimited, Alex?" he began.

"Not much," she admitted candidly. "I know you've been in this location for a couple of years. When you first opened up, there was an article in the paper..." She searched her memory fruitlessly for some recollection, but it evaded her. At the time, she had paid scant attention to the opening of a new business that didn't concern her. The Jameson clan made all their travel arrangements through the agency located in the bank they owned.

To her relief, Brian Campbell revealed neither surprise nor concern over her ignorance. He matter-of-factly informed her that Globe Travel Unlimited was a very large corporation with branch offices in cities all over the United States. The fundamental philosophy that made Globe different from other agencies was the premise that travel is not just for the wealthy.

"We make it possible for the ordinary person on a modest income to travel anywhere in the world," he said, warming to a subject he quite obviously enjoyed discussing. "We can do that because we're large and offer carefully planned tours based on our own research. We don't depend on hearsay or the advice of some so-called travel expert who hasn't been to a country for the past ten years."

His enthusiasm was contagious. Alex could feel excitement building inside her as she searched his explanation for some clue as to her own future employment. Because at this point she would just die from disappointment if he didn't hire her. His words had painted an alluring landscape of a world outside Stokely she longed to explore. When she could hardly restrain a second longer the urge to blurt "But what does all this have to do with *me*?" he smiled in a way that indicated awareness of her impatience.

"If you're really serious about your willingness to travel extensively, I'm prepared to offer you a job with Globe Travel. Your first assignment would be to research a tour to Portugal."

Alex's eyes widened as his words sank in. "*Portugal*," she breathed, at once besieged by doubts of her ability to perform the duties he had outlined. "But I've never been to Europe. I don't speak *any* Portuguese..." She trailed off in dismay.

"Don't worry," he reassured her. "We have no intention of just tossing you to the wolves. The main stockholder in Globe Travel, the guy who started the whole operation, is still very active in the business. If his schedule permits, he will meet you in Lisbon and train you personally. If not, one of our other training managers will take his place. After that, you'll come back here and do a stint of desk duty. Then in six months you'll have another travel assignment, this time with an experienced agent in the company. The way we work out the schedule, no agent is stuck behind the desk all the time."

"I don't know what to say," she said slowly, too overcome with the enormity of this development in her life to notice that he was watching her very closely or that his eyes held a trace of that same curiosity with which he had regarded her two days ago as he took her application. "Everything I want to say seems so—so trite and unoriginal. This job offer is like an answer to a prayer. A dream come true." She giggled, giving him a glimpse of a younger spirit beneath the well-groomed facade.

"You accept the offer?" he inquired, his businesslike manner restoring her poise.

"I accept the offer," she pronounced clearly, her mind racing madly with all the things she had to do. She would need a passport. There was shopping to be done too. But first she would go right out and buy some books on Portugal. Maybe she could even master a few phrases and words in Portuguese. That should impress this big boss with her aptitude for the job.

It took a real effort to concentrate on Brian Campbell's words until she realized he was telling her she had just three weeks in which to prepare herself for the trip. Three weeks! It was surely impossible to get everything done in that short a time!

But when she left the agency, she didn't embark on any of the errands she had such a limited time to accomplish. She went directly to the nearest telephone and dialed a familiar number.

"Jinx? Alex here. Jinx, you'll just *never* guess what's happened! Remember what we were talking about the other day over lunch?" Her voice was vibrant, alive, her features glowing with happiness while two large tears rolled down her cheeks. "Well, Jinx, you won't believe this. You just won't *believe*..."

Chapter Two

WARNED ABOUT THE horrors of jet lag, Alex tried, with little success, to sleep on the plane. There was too much going on: one meal hardly seemed over before the flight attendants were passing out the next one. And then there was the full-length movie which lasted two hours. But the main reason she hadn't slept was the most obvious one—she was too keyed up with excitement.

When she emerged from the plane and stood on the pavement with a group of other passengers waiting for a bus to transport them to the terminal, she was glad for the jacket of her spring suit. The brisk wind which tore at her hair and whipped her skirt around her legs had a bite surprising for the middle of June. Should she have brought warmer clothing?

13

Going through customs at the terminal was so perfunctory she was vaguely disappointed, having expected she knew not what exactly, but certainly a little more interest in her spanking new U.S. passport. Afterward, she found herself in a drab underground area near the luggage conveyor belt and stationed herself among the passengers waiting for their bags. Many of them had dollies, but she had packed light and would be able to carry her one bag and the overnight case and handbag she had brought with her on the plane.

Forty-five minutes later she was leaning wearily against a post, dizzy from watching the conveyor belt glide by with no sign of her cream-colored leather suitcase. Nearly all the other passengers were gone now, some of them pushing dollies piled high with incredibly strange assortments of huge bags bound up with rough twine, presumably to prevent their bursting open and spilling the contents. For a while she had been entertained by idle speculation: Who were these people? Where were they coming from? But the novelty of watching other passengers soon palled, and finally it dawned on her that all the luggage had been unloaded. Her bag had either been lost or left behind at Kennedy Airport in New York.

What a depressing way to begin her adventure in Portugal! For a moment she slumped under the weight of this awful development. Then she straightened her shoulders with determination. What kind of world traveler was she going to be if she let a mishap like this rattle her composure? It wasn't as if there were no stores in Lisbon. She wasn't penniless and at the mercy of the world.

No, but tiredness was creeping up on her now and it was an effort just to stand in line, waiting to report that her bag had not arrived with her on the flight. The young man behind the counter displayed a convincing concern and assured her the bag would be delivered to her hotel when it arrived.

Fortunately there was no long line at the currency exchange window, which was open even though it was

Sunday, and for a moment Alex forgot her fatigue in contemplation of the pile of escudo notes she received for her traveler's checks. It was very colorful money and not uniform in size like American dollars, yet the size of a note did not seem related to its value. It seemed more like Monopoly money than *real* currency!

All the taxis lined up at the curb were painted the same colors, black and aqua, though the automobiles themselves were of varying makes. The one she drew was not as new and clean as some of the others and the driver was noticeably unkempt, but she was unsure of how to indicate her wish for another taxi. Also she didn't want to make a serious blunder in protocol that might alienate all the drivers and leave her stranded there on the curb. How embarrassing *that* would be—if she had to be rescued from the airport.

Which reminded her that Brian Campbell had never gotten around to mentioning the name of the man who would train her, even though she had asked once or twice. Each time, Brian had remembered something important to tell her and she would forget again, having much more exciting things on her mind. Then the day before she was to leave, she had been more insistent.

"Who *is* this mystery man?" she demanded, half teasing and half serious. "Why won't you tell me his name?"

Brian had suddenly become totally absorbed in the search for some article in a drawer of his desk. "Er, I meant to tell you..." he said absently. "It looks now like Jim Tate, our regional manager out on the West Coast, *may* be the one to meet you in Lisbon. You'll like Jim..."

Brian had gone on to tell her a little about the man likely to be training her, and once again the whole subject of the boss was dropped. Alex still didn't know his name, but it no longer seemed important. She did find Brian's evasiveness puzzling though.

The taxi driver's handling of the car didn't raise her initial opinion of him. She had to brace herself as he sped around curves and screeched to a halt at traffic lights. It seemed to be taking a long time to get to her hotel, and she wondered worriedly if she was getting one of those classic long-way-around rides. Just when she was bordering on panic, he rounded a corner with squealing tires and braked to a halt, throwing her forward. He muttered something incomprehensible and pointed across the street.

Seeing the large block letters HOTEL JORGE across the front of a narrow building about five stories tall brought a flood of relief. He had at least brought her to the proper destination, or so it seemed. She noted with interest the small balconies overlooking the street.

"*Quanto custa?*" she enunciated carefully. Pride in her recall of the Portuguese phrase for "How much is it?" quickly faded into chagrin as he rattled off a reply she couldn't understand. The guidebooks mentioned a reasonably standard fee for taxi transport from the airport to the center of Lisbon, but she couldn't remember it right now, and for the first time she realized he hadn't switched on the mileage meter the way he should have. She dug out the pile of escudo notes from her handbag and looked at him helplessly.

"How much?" she asked meekly, abandoning the useless pretense of any understanding of the Portuguese language.

He repeated the same unintelligible sounds, this time with undisguised impatience, all the while eyeing the escudo notes in her hand with greed.

In desperation she dug again into her handbag and unearthed a pen and piece of paper. Using sign language, she motioned him to write down the charge. The symbol for escudo was, she knew, identical to that for dollar but was written after the price rather than before it.

He slashed something across the paper and thrust it back at her. The initial digit could have been a three or a five—she couldn't be sure since his handwriting was no better than his driving or his manners. She handed him a five-hundred escudo note (500$), unable at that moment to remember how much it was worth in American money.

He grabbed the note, threw up his hands in disgust, and unleashed a tirade that held a distinct undertone of violence. *Now* what was the matter, she wondered desperately, cowering back against the dusty seat. After a prolonged pantomine on his part, she ascertained that he apparently did not have the proper change.

At this point Alex would have been willing to part with the whole stack of escudo notes just to escape the brutish lout. She searched her brain for "It's all right" in Portuguese.

"*Muito bem.* Don't worry about the change, *keep it!* Thank you—er, *obrigado.*"

She opened her own door and stumbled out of the car. Her face must have reflected her distress when she walked into the small old-fashioned entrance of the hotel because the hall porter who greeted her from behind the counter was solicitous in his manner. It took a few seconds for her to comprehend *why* she had understood every single word he said.

"Thank God! You speak English!" she breathed, walking over to the counter and leaning her elbows on it, needing the support because her legs felt strangely rubbery. "I just had the most ghastly experience."

His face grew sternly disapproving as she recounted what had happened. "He overcharged you," he said, shaking his head. "The standard fee is one hundred escudos. I regret you had such an unfortunate introduction to Portugal, mademoiselle. Most of our taxi drivers are very honest. Only a few, like this scoundrel, give the others a bad reputation."

Alex no longer cared. She was just greatly relieved to find herself safe at the hotel in the reassuring presence of someone who spoke such good English. She suffered one more moment of anxiety as he checked the register for her name, but miraculously it was there and she *did* have a reservation. The way her luck was going today, she wouldn't have been surprised to find herself out on the street with no place to sleep.

"If you will be so kind as to leave your passport with me, the bellboy will show you to your room." He gestured to a young boy dressed in skin-tight black slacks and a white shirt.

At the last moment Alex remembered something and turned back toward the desk. "Has anyone, a man named Jim Tate, left a message for me?"

"Ah, mademoiselle, yes! Forgive me!"

She smiled, waving away the apology as the man rushed over to her with a folded note in hand. She wondered irrelevantly why a Portuguese would address an American with a French courtesy title. Was it because the French language had been universal in Europe for so many years? She forgot that speculation as she glanced down at the message.

The few words in bold masculine script were scrawled on Globe Travel Unlimited stationery: *Meet me in lobby at eight P.M. for dinner, please. V. R.* The *please* somewhat softened that peremptory message which, obviously, was not from the West Coast manager, Jim Tate. Was she to be trained by the boss of Globe Travel after all? Tonight she would learn the answer to that question, but right now she was simply too exhausted to care who V. R. was. The long wait for her lost luggage, the awful taxi driver, and the sleepless night full of restless excitement had taken a toll. Even though it was scarcely mid-morning, she longed for her bed.

She was delighted with the cleanliness and charm of her small room. The sheets on the narrow twin beds were dazzling white, crackling with starch, and ever so inviting! The bathroom fixtures were of old-fashioned porcelain and gleamed from scrubbing. The tub was gigantic, deeper and longer by far than its modern counterpart in American homes and hotels. She delayed exploring her room, particularly the little balcony, in favor of a long soak in the huge tub. Half an hour later, Alex slid in between the deliciously smooth ironed sheets, her body utterly relaxed.

Hours later when the alarm clock shrilled, she was shocked to see that the precaution of setting it had been necessary after all. She had slept the day away, and she had only one hour to rid herself of the puffy-eyed consequences of jet lag and prepare for her dinner with the mysterious V. R.

She took a great deal of care with her appearance and was pleased with what the mirror showed. She was glad she had traveled in her nicest suit since she had nothing to change into. It looked like linen, but was a true miracle fabric that didn't wrinkle. Its topaz color was highly becoming, harmonizing with the honey tones of her hair and eyes. Sandals in a contrasting darker brown were elegant without being frivolous, the moderate heels adding an additional two inches to her above-average height.

Curiosity intermingled with faint but understandable apprehension as she stepped out of the tiny elevator into the lobby. She had been so excited about this trip to Portugal she hadn't dwelled on the possibility that she might *not* measure up to the demands of this job. What if this Mr. V. R., whoever he was, didn't like her? Suppose he found her lacking the qualities he desired in an employee? Jobs like this one certainly wouldn't be easy to find if this one fell through.

Faced with these daunting specters of failure, she hardly glanced at the dark-haired man seated on a sofa across the room from the reception desk. The person she was looking for should be at least in his fifties, quite possibly with graying hair. But there wasn't anyone else in the lobby except the hall porter and a bellboy, both behind the counter, herself, and the man, who tossed his magazine onto the low table in front of him and stood up, causing her to flick her eyes back in his direction.

An intuitively feminine part of her mind registered his height, which was well above average, and the lean

muscular build under superbly fitting slacks and jacket.
Then recognition hit as her eyes met his squarely for the
first time. She stared, grappling with a conclusion that
couldn't possibly be true. The representative of Globe
Travel she was meeting *couldn't be*—but the initials fit!

"Vince Reardon," she managed to get out finally, and
then found herself once again incapable of coherent
speech. Her confusion just wouldn't coalesce into a statement or a question. In contrast to her own shattered
composure, he was utterly poised, his gaze taking her
in from head to toe, missing nothing in her appearance.

When her mind began to work again with some measure of clarity, she realized that he must have known all
along who *she* was. Had he deliberately withheld his
own identity when he signed only his initials to the note?
But why...

"You know all the time who I was?" Accusation struggled with disbelief in her voice, as memories came rushing back.

"How many Alex Jamesons are there in Stokely, Georgia?" he countered, thrusting his hands into the pockets
of his well-cut trousers and closing the distance between
them.

No wonder she hadn't recognized him immediately.
It was hard to believe this was the same Vince Reardon
she had known seven years ago. Not that he had aged
to disadvantage or changed noticeably in physique. He
had been as tall and lean and athletically fit then as he
was now, and his dark hair didn't have a trace of gray.
But there was an inbred self-assurance, a patina of success, an aloofness, too, that the younger Vince had definitely lacked.

"Are you? I mean, you're *not*..." she floundered
confusedly.

"I'm the founder and primary stockholder in Globe
Travel Unlimited," he said quietly, somehow divining
the question she struggled to ask.

"But *why*, if you *knew* who I was all the time—"

He smiled crookedly, in a way that *was* familiar, reviving a long forgotten awareness of his masculinity. "I'd be a hell of a businessman and even less of a person if I held a grudge because you turned me down in favor of a better marriage prospect."

Her eyes dropped from his. If only it were the way he made it sound, so casually simple, cut and dried. Mortification welled inside her, heightening the color in her cheeks, as she recalled in appalling clarity their parting seven years ago. The things she had *said* to him! How could he forgive her?

"There's plenty of time to scare up old ghosts. Do you feel up to walking a few blocks or would you prefer a taxi?" he asked matter-of-factly.

She wanted—no, needed—to walk. They passed the Marques de Pombal monument and stopped at the Fenix Hotel.

"The Bodegon Room here is excellent without being overpriced," he commented, guiding her down a flight of stairs from the street and into a small restaurant in the basement of the hotel. It had the quietly understated atmosphere of a tavern, the low white ceiling crossed with dark varnished beams. The tables were draped in crisp white linen and set with an impressive array of heavy silver that had seen much use.

On the way to the restaurant there had been surprisingly little awkwardness between them. Vince had questioned her about her flight and her activities since arrival in Lisbon, expressing sympathy over the missing bag and seemingly not in the least disturbed by her difficulty in coping with the gouging methods of the taxi driver.

"In the future, insist the meter be turned on right at the beginning. If you still suspect you're being overcharged, demand to be taken to the police station. You'll be surprised at the change that takes place then," he advised. "Southern European countries are eager to encourage tourism to boost their economies. The last thing the authorities want is for visitors to feel abused."

Seated across from him in the restaurant, a thickly
bound menu open in front of her, Alex took advantage
of an opportunity to observe Vince while his attention
was concentrated on a conversation with the maître
d'hôtel, a pompous little man who introduced himself
as Philippe. Vince couldn't really be called handsome,
she decided. His features were too aggressively masculine, the square chin and firm mouth suggesting flinty
determination. His hair was crisp and thick and, like his
eyes, almost black. Looking at him now, easily the most
impressive man in the room, it was impossible to believe
that once she, an eighteen-year-old schoolgirl at the time,
had ruled over him like an apprentice Cleopatra.

Pushing aside that thought and the others it brought
in its wake, she told him her choice of food as if she had
actually been studying the menu instead of him. She had
a cold appetizer, *sardines en tomato*; cream of asparagus
soup, creamy and delicate; and paella, a spicy concoction
of shellfish and rice.

In her opinion, the high reputation of the restaurant
was well deserved. The food was delicious, the Portuguese wine Vince chose, a white Colares, was excellent,
and the service quite exceeded anything to which Alex
was accustomed, even in good restaurants in Atlanta.
They had no fewer than four people waiting on them,
ostensibly devoted to their well-being during the meal:
Philippe, a wine steward, and two waiters.

During dinner the conversation centered around the
purpose of their presence in Lisbon. Alex's confidence
blossomed as Vince explained what they would be doing
during the next two weeks. They would see as much, do
as much, as possible, keeping in mind at all times the
objective of experiencing the most for their money, cutting corners in ways that wouldn't diminish their enjoyment of what the area offered.

"The old argument 'you get what you pay for' may
be true," Vince said with a dismissive shrug. "But if you
can't afford the Ritz route, which requires no imagination

whatever, I'm convinced you can get *more* than you pay for. In the long run the sense of adventure and resourcefulness may even compensate for whatever one is denied in luxury."

"Not only is the idea behind your travel agency clever," Alex praised, "but it's humanitarian." She bristled to cover her embarrassment as he shot her a skeptical look. "Of course the end result is profit for you and the business, but you still provide a very worthwhile service for a lot of people," she insisted doggedly.

They both were silent during the brief time required for the waiters to clear the table and serve tiny cups of thick black coffee, neither of them choosing dessert from the sumptuous choices on the cart wheeled up to the table. When they were alone again, Alex was overwhelmed with questions that opened up a past undoubtedly painful to him and acutely embarrassing to her.

"We might as well talk about it," he said bluntly, taking her by surprise and demonstrating that he must have read her mind. "Otherwise we won't be able to work together. Item number one: your turning me down flat in favor of Courtney Jameson was the biggest favor anyone ever did for me."

Alex was utterly flabbergasted. Whatever she might have expected or hoped or dreaded to hear, it certainly wasn't this. She listened with wide-eyed attention as he continued.

"I don't deny that my ego was badly bruised at the time, but you made me realize I was headed nowhere by staying in the military. Without a college degree, there was a limit to the promotions I could expect. When my second term was up, a few months after I was home on leave and met you, I didn't reenlist as I'd intended to do."

She made a little utterance of protest, covering her face with both hands. The memory of her eighteen-year-old candor made her cringe now. She had made it explicitly clear to Vince Reardon, home on leave to visit the widowed mother whose main support he provided, that he didn't measure up to what she wanted in a husband. He lacked sophistication and social background, which she deemed necessary for the kind of success her husband would have to have. How ironic those words were now in view of what had happened to both of them in the intervening years.

The man across from her laughed softly. "You sure didn't pull your punches."

She dropped her hands and eyed him in surprise. As far as she could tell, there wasn't a trace of rancor in his voice or features. Could it be true that he *didn't* hold a grudge, that he *didn't* despise her for her youthful cruelty?

"Oh God," she murmured, unable herself to restrain a note of bitterness over the past. "What a shallow, vain little fool I was. You'd have to be a saint not to feel a little vindictive the way things have turned out." She overruled his gesture of protest. "No, I insist. I want to tell you. In a way I *owe* it to you after the way I—"

"I'm aware that you're divorced," he interrupted quietly.

"What you may *not* know," she continued bleakly, "is that you're a bigger success in every way than Courtney, with all the advantages of his wealthy background. He doesn't even support himself. He spends the majority of his time, when he isn't on a 'business trip,' out on the golf course. I think his father finally gave up on the hope that his only son would be able to take over the Jameson business interests."

Alex found talking about her dissolved marriage, particularly the last two years, painful but she felt compelled to tell Vince in some detail what a failure she had been, as though that confession might compensate in some small measure for the harshness of her treatment of him seven years earlier. She told him of how she had never really felt accepted by Courtney's friends, even though she had tried her best at first to excel in bridge and tennis and cocktail party conversation.

Vince listened, showing little reaction and saying nothing until she had talked herself out. "I see. Being a society matron didn't measure up to your expectations. Yet you didn't have children?"

Pain darkened her eyes until they were almost the color of her suit. "I didn't measure up to the Jameson standard there either," she said bleakly. "In the long run, it was probably all for the best. A marriage has to have more than children to cement it together."

Vince motioned to the waiter to refill their coffee cups and ordered cognac for them both without even consulting her. By the time he transferred his attention back to her, she had regained her composure.

"So," she began with an effort at lightness that missed the mark, "that's the depressing little tale of my one and only venture into matrimony. The adage 'live and learn' should be reversed in my case. I've learned all I ever want to know about marriage and now I'm ready to live. What about you, Vince? Are you married?" She looked at his left hand, which bore no wedding ring.

"No, I am not now nor have I been married. There really hasn't been time. And in today's society, a man has little reason to bind himself legally to a woman unless—"

"Unless he wants children," Alex completed for him, her chest constricting oddly. A man like Vince would want children eventually, she knew. He had been an only child reared by his mother on the small income she earned as a janitoress on the staff of one of the public schools in Stokely. Now that he was a financial success, he would want heirs to share in his pride and accomplishment.

"My father will be very proud to hear about you," she said thoughtfully, too engrossed in the sequence of her own reflections to notice the guarded expression that settled over Vince's features. Her father had taught Vince in high school and apparently had been a steadying influence on him during some trying years. She had met

Vince in her own senior year of high school, when he called on her father at their home, as many of his students did in the years following their graduation.

He had asked Alex to go out with him, and she had been very flattered to have an "older man" pay attention to her. Looking back now, she realized how much trust her father must have placed in Vince to permit her to date a man eight years her senior. But soon after that, Courtney Jameson had arrived home from college during a holiday break, or so he had told her at the time, and she had been too dazzled with his sleek sports car and glib sophistication to give Vince the time of day. Beside the Jameson heir, he had paled into utter insignificance. Later when she learned the truth, that Courtney had been asked to leave the university for numerous violations of the regulations, it hardly seemed important. Why would someone in Courtney's position need a college degree?

Now that Alex had told Vince about her own past, she had numerous questions about his life during the years since she had seen him last. In an abbreviated fashion he told her of holding various jobs, of several different efforts to go into business for himself, making some fortunate contacts in the process. One of those contacts had backed him financially when he decided to buy a struggling little agency in New Orleans that specialized in guided tours of the city. That had been the unlikely beginning of what now was Globe Travel Unlimited.

"It's surprising I didn't *know* about you," she said in puzzlement, wrinkling her brow.

"There's no reason you should," he contradicted. "Stokely isn't really that small, and I spend very little time there."

A horrible thought occurred to Alex. "Vince, you didn't think—"

He smiled the charming crooked smile. "No, Alex, I didn't suspect you of trying to capitalize on an old infatuation. If I had any suspicion you knew of my association with Globe Travel, you certainly dispelled it when you saw me in the lobby tonight."

The reply answered more than one of Alex's questions. He *had* deliberately withheld his identity from her, obviously as a kind of test. Considering the past, she couldn't blame him. On the contrary, she had to believe it very decent of him not to hold the past against her, as he seemed not to do.

With the check paid, he escorted her outside, more intent now on the future than the past. During the walk back to the Hotel Jorge, he outlined their activities for the following day. The touch of his hand on her arm was that of a courteous escort, but she could feel the warmth of his flesh through the linen fabric of her jacket, and she became increasingly aware of the tall masculine figure striding with such muscular ease beside her.

When the hotel was in sight, just half a block away, she was unable to listen to him. Would he, like so many men, feel bound to test out the popular myth about divorced women, that they were sex-starved and would willingly climb into bed with a man at the slightest provocation?

To complicate matters further, he *was* her boss now, and she wouldn't want to do anything to offend him and maybe jeopardize her job, which she wanted more than ever after tonight. The only answer was to meet any advances from him with firm, polite refusal. She had made this decision by the time they entered the lobby of the hotel and crossed over to the elevator.

Her unease strengthened to unreasoning panic during the short ascent to her floor. She could only blame the cramped confines of the tiny elevator for the inescapable blanket of intimacy which enclosed them. To avoid eye contact, she busied herself with digging inside her handbag for the key she had forgotten to leave at the desk, according to the European custom. She felt rather than saw the searching look from the tall man beside her as the silence between them hung taut. A faint masculine scent, clean and spicy and tantalizingly blended with the warmth of hard male flesh, assailed her nostrils, increasing her awareness of him as a virile man and at the same time arousing in her body an answering response independent of the workings of her mind.

By the time the elevator jerked to a standstill, in that halting manner of an absent-minded old man, Alex could actually feel her pulsebeat. At the door of her room, she turned to Vince with the kind of brittle cocktail party smile she had learned to cultivate after she became Mrs. Courtney Jameson.

"Goodnight, Vince. I truly enjoyed the evening. This is my idea of a perfect job—a marvelous dinner in good company and then the luxury of a room I don't have to share with anyone."

His eyes narrowed, the withdrawal in him something she sensed rather than actually saw. Her message had come through all right, but she felt about as subtle as a flashing neon sign. And deep down, there was the nagging suspicion she might have wronged him again, since nothing in his manner or his conversation during the evening could be construed as preliminary groundwork for the seduction of his employee. She wished desperately she could retract the prim, set little speech and start all over again.

"Wasn't there *anything* about marriage you liked, Alex?" he asked softly, and the astuteness of the question slashed to the core of her apprehensions, which went much deeper than worrying about her reputation.

She sagged back against the wooden panels of the door, thrown off guard. "Such a horrid word, *frigid*, and such an affront to the red-blooded American husband." Her low voice was hoarse with bitterness and shame.

"Perhaps that's because he knows deep down there's an inadequate man for every cold woman."

A lazy note in the deep voice shivered along her spine, making every cell in her body come tingling alive as if she had been administered a small electric shock. At that moment she more than halfway hoped he would disregard her keep-off sign. He had changed in so many ways. Something told her the clumsy passionate kisses she had only tolerated years ago might have been refined too, like his whole self-confident bearing. The thought was intriguing.

He took the large old-fashioned key from her tense fingers, fitted it into the lock, and pushed open the door. "Goodnight, Alex. If your luggage hasn't arrived by morning, we'll have to get you some shoes more suitable for walking than those," he said briskly and was gone before she could summon a word.

Chapter Three

ALEX JERKED UPRIGHT in bed, totally disoriented as she gazed around the strange room with sleep-glazed eyes. *Where was she*? Then simultaneously came a repetition of the two sounds which had awakened her. A loud knocking at the door, this time accompanied by a strident female voice, and the abrupt, nerve-jangling noise from the telephone situated on the table between the two twin beds.

Unable to respond to both summonses at the same time, she did nothing for several seconds until comprehension cleared her fuzziness. She reached over and picked up the telephone receiver, managed a husky "Thank you," and then swung out of bed and went swiftly to the door, opening it a narrow crack.

Outside stood a burly woman in maid's uniform so impeccably starched and ironed it might have stood by

itself. She held a tray laden with a steaming coffee pot
and breakfast service. Her face beamed with open good
humor when she saw Alex peering out at her.

"*Ola!*" she boomed cheerfully. "*Pequeno almoço,
señorita.*"

Puzzled, Alex swung open the door to admit her. She
could see for herself it was breakfast, or *pequeno almoço*
in Portuguese, but did the Hotel Jorge serve breakfast
to all its patrons in their rooms at 7:30 A.M.?

The woman spoke a cheerful stream of Portuguese
Alex assumed to be stock pleasantries such as comments
on the weather. After depositing the tray on a low table
near the glass doors leading to the little balcony, she
stood for a moment with her blunt-tipped hands folded
across her ample middle, smiling and regarding Alex
with a trace of expectancy. Then she turned and started
to leave the room.

"Wait! Please!" Alex made a dive for her purse, remembering finally what she had read in her guidebooks
on Portugal. Domestic workers such as maids in hotels
made very low wages and were customarily given a small
tip for satisfactory service.

"Here. Thank you very much. *Obrigado!*"

"*Obrigado! Obrigado, señorita!*" The woman took
the coin and rewarded Alex with a shy but happy smile
as she left.

It was only when she was alone, seated in a low
armchair beside the table, that she saw the note. Of
course! Why hadn't she realized immediately that Vince
must be responsible for this unaccustomed luxury of
breakfast served in her room?

Delight at his thoughtfulness made her curve her lips
into a soft little smile as she opened the note. Disappointingly, it was nothing more than news from Vince
that her bag had arrived at the airport and was on its way
to the hotel. His request that she meet him in the lobby
in an hour seemed stiff and formal.

But he was a considerate man, she reflected, pouring

thick black coffee into a cup and diluting it with an equal amount of boiled milk. The breakfast was continental style, as she expected—no bacon, eggs, hash brown potatoes, or grits. There was an appetizing assortment of rolls, ample servings of real butter, marmelade, and fruit preserves. She enjoyed the simple elegance of the meal, appreciative that the napkins were linen, not paper, and that care had been taken to arrange the tray attractively, to please the eye as well as the palate.

Just as she was finishing a second cup of coffee, a youthful bellboy delivered her bag to the door. Remembering Vince's parting comment last night about wearing shoes suitable for walking, she dressed in tailored brown slacks, a long-sleeved shirt blouse in crisp brown-and-white-striped cotton, and crepe-soled brown leather shoes. Before leaving the room, she draped a white cardigan around her shoulders.

"Good girl," Vince approved when they met downstairs, his dark eyes taking in every aspect of her appearance. "You'll probably need that sweater the first couple of hours this morning."

She glowed in response to that frankly admiring inspection. His own attire was casual, slacks, shirt, and a lightweight jacket he had left unbuttoned, but Alex noted again the easy distinction with which he wore his clothes.

"Thanks for ordering breakfast served in my room," she said as soon as they were out of the hotel. Striding along in the fresh morning air, she was grateful for her sweater; it was chilly in spite of the brilliance of the sunshine. Before he could even reply, though, she told him of her waking confusion and erroneous conclusion that everyone in the hotel was automatically served breakfast at seven-thirty in the morning.

"It was really sweet of you to think of it," she ended, smiling up at him.

"Don't mention it," he said casually. "I forgot to remind you last night that breakfast is included with the room—'bed and breakfast,' it's called over here. And it's quite acceptable to ask to have it served in your room, not a special luxury as it would be considered in the States."

He had laughed with genuine amusement at her deliberately comic account of her ignorance of European hotel procedure, but now he sounded absent-minded as he spoke, giving more attention to their surroundings than to her. She was reminded, somewhat to her irritation, that he was her boss and for him this was just another working day.

His offhand attitude dimmed the glow she had felt ever since the discovery of his note on her breakfast tray. He had made it clear that what he did for her he would have done for any new employee in her position. She would have to be careful after this not to jump to conclusions about his actions, she admonished herself stiffly.

Before long she had completely forgotten her recent intention to remain reserved, so fascinated was she with the old section of Lisbon through which they were walking in order to reach their immediate destination, St. George's Castle or Castelo de São Jorge, as the Portuguese called it. Located as it was up on a hill above the city, it was a visible reminder of Lisbon's antiquity.

Alex had never walked on streets so incredibly narrow and steep and irregular. The cobbled pavement presented unfamiliar hazards, especially to someone like herself— too interested in trying to see everything to watch where she was stepping. Vince grabbed her arm several times to prevent her from stumbling into the path of a vehicle or colliding with hurrying pedestrians, and after a while he maintained a firm, steadying grip.

He seemed as interested as she in the quaint old buildings with lacy wrought-iron balconies and showed no impatience at her frequent pauses and excited exclamations over what she saw. At the top of one long alleyway, which was nothing more than a steep staircase between buildings, they came to a two-story concrete building oddly out of place in its surroundings. Entering the stark, ugly structure, they discovered it to be a huge food market on two levels, the whole center of the building a large square opening to admit light and air.

Individuals manned stalls offering a wide variety of fruits and vegetables, and there was a great deal of loud haggling over prices between buyers and sellers. One display drew Alex's horrified attention. Freshly plucked chickens were piled high on trays, the heads and horny clawed feet still on the carcasses. A little further on, a woman sold fresh sardines whose shiny color made them look artificial, like oiled aluminum foil.

As much as Alex hated to admit her weakness, she found the combined odors of the market overpowering and was beginning to feel a little faint when Vince led her outside, where she hastily gulped a breath of fresh air.

"Not the kind of supermarket we're used to," he commented wryly, making her realize she hadn't done a creditable job of hiding her reaction from him.

"Somehow it didn't look terribly sterile," she admitted a trifle hesitantly, not wanting to sound narrow-minded and squeamish.

They had begun walking again, but not very fast. The pitch of the street was extremely steep, so she was frankly grateful for the support of his arm around her shoulders, steadying her.

"Even though Lisbon is a modern city in many ways, a lot of the people still don't have refrigeration in their homes and have to go to market every day for their food," he explained.

They had already passed numerous women, many of whom were dressed entirely in black, with small plastic bags of fresh produce or fish or small, unidentifiable cuts of meat. Alex soon surmised that at least in this section of town it was the usual practice for a shopper to bring her own carrier, be it basket or the less picturesque but undeniably more practical plastic bag.

"Not much farther now," Vince assured just as Alex's heel again found a large crevice in the cobblestones and her ankle twisted awkwardly under her. "Here, hang on to me," he ordered, and before she could acquiesce or protest, he had taken her hand which had clutched at him and slid it around his waist under the jacket.

Just as he had promised, it wasn't long before they arrived at the entrance gates of the castle. Alex had spent the entire time debating with herself, torn between chagrin at her own deplorable lack of ruggedness and a totally inconsistent urge to lean on his masculine strength. His body was firm under her arm, the muscles under his shirt flexing with each movement. She could have walked all day in that close, strong embrace.

The thought brought a guilty flush to her cheeks as she realized she had once again lapsed into thinking of Vince not as her employer but as a male companion, a very attractive and compelling one too. Self-consciousness made her pull away from him, even though the terrain inside the castle walls was far from smooth. He released her immediately, arousing a flare of resentment in Alex that their close physical contact obviously had not affected him as it had her.

She walked with great care over stones and up and down crude steps, determined to prove she was completely capable of getting along without his assistance. As if sensing her prickly independence, he made no offer to take her arm as they explored the gardens of the castle and then climbed a rude stone staircase up to the ramparts.

"Oh!" she breathed. "How magnificent!"

They stood side by side gazing at the spectacular panoramic view of the city of Lisbon bordered by the wide, curving band of the Tagus River. The clay tile roofs formed a vivid mosaic of shades of orange which contrasted charmingly with the blue of the river, the rich, verdant green of vegetation, and the buff and oyster-white sides of the buildings.

"We came from right down there." Vince pointed out a landmark below them in the maze of narrow, twisting streets and tall, steep-roofed buildings of the Alfama, the oldest section of the city. "It should take an able-winged bird at least one minute to get where we are, and we took—let's see—almost two hours!"

The friendly teasing note was back in his deep voice. Alex's heart expanded with joy as she met the laughter gleaming in his dark eyes. At that moment she was intensely happy to be here at this glorious spot in the world at this particular time in history with—yes, she might as well complete the thought since she was thinking it—with this very likable man.

The radiant smile she cast up at him mirrored the elation welling inside her, making her feel weightless and carefree. The curve of her lips, the golden light shining in her eyes, invited him to share the overwhelming exhilaration she felt.

"This sounds silly, I know—the kind of thing you don't say *out loud*!" she exclaimed softly, a note of exultance in her voice. "But right now I almost *feel* like a bird about to take off and soar above the earth—*free*!"

For one breathless moment she watched something flare up in his eyes, some inexplicable emotion that only compounded her excitement, and then it was gone and she was left to wonder if it hadn't been just her overwrought imagination. His lips twisted in a rueful smile just before he turned brusquely away from her, so that she couldn't tell what his expression was.

"Don't get any ideas about taking a short cut back down or Globe Travel will be short one employee," he said lightly, starting back down the stone steps, leaving her no choice but to follow.

Parked in the courtyard just inside the entrance gates of the castle was a taxi, readily identifiable as such because of its distinctive aqua-and-black color scheme. The driver lounged against the hood, smoking a cigarette in

the style Alex associated with gangsters in old Humphrey
Bogart movies.

Perceiving Vince's intentions as he headed directly
for the taxi, she couldn't hold back a burning protest.
Since they had climbed down from the ramparts he had
said scarcely twenty words, and these were all responses
to comments or questions from her. What had she done
or said up there to bring about this mood of deep seriousness? Had she been so naive in her exuberance that
he was now sorry Brian Campbell had hired her? Was
he planning to hire a taxi to take her directly back to the
hotel?

"Vince, please! Wait a minute!"

In her desperation she grasped his arm to force him
to stop. It turned to steel under her fingers as she clung
to him, inner turmoil clearly reflected in her features as
she gazed up questioningly at him.

"The taxi...why are you—I mean, aren't we supposed to walk?" She wet her dry lips nervously with the
tip of her tongue, not even conscious she was doing so
until his gaze dropped to watch the quick motion. She
wished fervently he would *say* something, not just look
at her as if he were trying to figure out where he had
seen her before.

Then to her immeasurable relief, he laughed, covering
the fingers clutching his arm with his own free hand. His
explanation held no trace of condescension.

"Alex, taxi fares in Portugal are extremely reasonable.
Only the real die-hard traveler or one with unlimited time
can afford not to take advantage of them."

She frowned in puzzlement. "Then why did we walk
up here?"

"Because we couldn't possibly have gotten the *feel*
of the old part of the city from an automobile, and that's
a great deal of what travel is about, isn't it?"

Relief shone in Alex's eyes at the reasonableness of
his explanation, transforming their color into clear golden

topaz. Thankful that he had dropped the distant manner
and seemed friendly again, she withdrew her hand with
the greatest reluctance from the warm strength of his.

How different this taxi ride was from that disastrous
first one! She thought about this for a moment with
amusement and immediately shared it with Vince. Alex
sat back and enjoyed the leisurely tour, exclaiming again
and again over the lovely old azulejos, or tiles, covering
whole walls and facades of buildings in the older sections
of town. Vince explained that the tiles were a part of the
Moorish influence on Portugal.

"Wait until you see the ones in southern Spain." His
casual comment made her heart beat faster at the assumption that this trip would certainly not be her last.

They ordered lunch at a small sidewalk cafe, and spent
the minutes before they were served jotting down comments and charting their earlier walking route on a large
map of Lisbon. As a reference they used the smaller map
Vince had marked on their way up to the castle.

"Some hardy souls will prefer to find their own way,"
he murmured absently.

Alex was strongly conscious of his head close to hers
and the distractingly masculine scent of him she drew
into her lungs with every breath. Several times her attention wandered from the conversation as she found
herself watching in fascination his long, supple fingers
moving across the map. His hands were so sure, so
strong, and yet so sensitive they intrigued her.

After lunch they walked through the Rossio district,
the business hub of downtown Lisbon, to the Praça do
Commercio, commonly called Black Horse Square because of the monument of that description. Elegantly
facaded government buildings surrounded the huge
square on three sides, while the fourth was open to the
busy activity of the harbor.

City buses arrived and departed at frequent intervals,
some of them green double-deckers straight out of a
London postcard, a fact not surprising when Alex learned

they were imported from England. After studying a large map covering the inside wall of a sidewalk bus-stop shelter, Alex and Vince were able to determine which buses would take them to the Belem suburb, where they would spend the afternoon.

Alex knew from her own research that Belem was very rich in history, offering many monuments to Portugal's Age of Exploration. Their first stop was the Tower of Belem, erected in the early sixteenth century on or near the spot where many of the famous expeditions set out.

"So this is the so-called Manueline style of architecture," Vince commented thoughtfully. He looked down at Alex's upturned face as she stared at the small square structure which had to be entered by a drawbridge that spanned the moat surrounding it. "What do you think of it?"

"It certainly is elaborate!" Her voice and face reflected frank amazement at the lavish decorative detail on the facade of the tower, an outlandish blend of Gothic and Romanesque. What engaged her attention at the moment, though, far more than this landmark to history, was the weight of Vince's arm thrown familiarly across her shoulders. She was almost afraid to breathe for fear he would wrongly think she objected to his touch. Because she certainly didn't.

As the afternoon progressed and they trekked from one historical monument to the next—ranging from the venerable old Jeronimos Monastery, its southern doorway the very ultimate in flamboyant Manueline fantasy, to the twentieth-century Memorial to the Discoveries, shaped like a prow of a ship about to embark on a voyage—Alex maintained a dialogue with herself. One she spoke aloud to Vince, while the other she spoke silently to herself.

What do you want from Vince? a little voice nagged repeatedly at her. *I just want him to be aware of me as a woman*, she snapped back defensively but refused

steadfastly to elaborate for the benefit of the irritating
little devil's advocate in her head. At this point she really
didn't *know* what she wanted from Vince, but she was
increasingly conscious of his compelling virility.

Gone now was the former reticence that precluded
physical contact between them. It seemed entirely natural
for Vince to hold her hand as they loped across a busy
street, and more often than not to retain it in a loose
grasp once they were safely on the opposite sidewalk.
The guiding pressure of his hand on the small of her
back, or at the trim curve of her waist, the sheltering
framework of his arm around her shoulders in a crowd,
these light touches could not in honesty be construed as
anything more than casual courtesy—or at the most ca-
maraderie—but they awoke a strong urge in Alex to
prolong and transform them into something more intimate.

She was far too intelligent not to perceive the irony
in her dissatisfaction with Vince's treatment of her as a
working partner. Considering her initial worries—could
that be only last night?—she should be pleased. But she
wasn't.

By the time they climbed down from the bus depositing them at the Praça Marques de Pombal, just a few
blocks from their hotel and now already grown familiar
to Alex, her feet were dragging so much that placing one
in front of the other required conscious effort. "After
today I may never walk again," she groaned wearily a
few minutes later as they crossed the hotel lobby to the
elevator.

"In that case it's a good thing we're going to a fado
club tonight. You probably don't feel like dancing anyway." Vince smiled down sympathetically at her as she
sagged against the polished steel of the elevator wall.
"You have several hours to rest up between now and
dinner. The fado music doesn't even start until ten, and
it lasts until dawn in some of the clubs."

At that moment Alex was unable to muster any enthusiasm for going out, but almost three hours later she awoke from a nap surprised to learn she had fallen asleep almost immediately after lying down and she now looked forward to the evening ahead. Feeling refreshed after a leisurely bath in the enormous old tub, she stood in a brief lace bra and panties in front of the closet deliberating over what to wear. The dress she slid off the hanger was one guaranteed to make Vince notice her. She had come close to not bringing it at all but at the last minute had tucked it into the suitcase since it was crushproof and took up little space, and she just *might* need a sophisticated black dress.

Examining herself critically in the mirror when she was dressed and hair and make-up had been attended to with painstaking care, she was seized with doubt at the wisdom of her choice. Was it too...too *brazen* and obvious? It clung seductively to the slender curves of her figure and the vee neckline plunged daringly to reveal the shadowy hollow between her breasts.

Her self-examination was interrupted by a light knock on the door. It was definitely too late to change now— Vince was outside, ready to escort her down to the lobby.

"Are you...ready?" He paused mid-question as she opened the door and stood in full view, steeling herself for his reaction. He looked even taller and more ruggedly masculine than she remembered in a dark tailored suit which fit his broad shoulders perfectly.

"I see you *are* ready," he said softly, taking a half step backward and thrusting his hands into the pockets of his trousers. His narrowed eyes moved slowly over her, pausing an extra fraction of a second at the exposed curve of her breasts.

She resisted a strong impulse to place a hand over the deep vee and forced her eyes to meet and hold his. "Is this dress too—too..." Her voice trailed off deliberately, challenging him to make his own interpretation.

"It is unquestionably *too—too*," he mocked lightly, his mouth twisting into the charmingly lopsided smile.

"If you're not careful, you'll upstage the celebrity singer at the O'Faia Club, and I understand she can be a bit temperamental."

The awkward moment passed. Vince's manner was urbane and imperturbable, but for Alex the success of having ruffled his implacable poise, even briefly, was sweet. The taxi ride to the popular club in the Bairro Alto section of Lisbon was charged with an electricity of mutual awareness that added keenly to Alex's pleasure in his company.

A uniformed doorman stood at the entrance of the O'Faia Club on a narrow, steeply-pitched street. Passing through a long dim passageway, they came into a small lounge with a large U-shaped banquette upholstered in shiny red vinyl, several small tables in front of it, and a bar placed against the inside wall.

Following the waiter's suggestion, they sat down on the banquette behind one of the tiny tables and ordered glasses of white port while they waited to be shown to their table in the next room.

"Hmm—delicious," Alex approved when she tasted the pale golden wine served in delicate faceted crystal glasses. As the waiter had promised, it wasn't at all cloying and sweet the way most people expected port to be.

She looked around with interest at the low beamed ceiling, the starkly white plaster walls whose thickness was evident in the arch leading from the lounge into the dining room beyond.

"Is fado strictly for the benefit of the tourists?" The question, spoken in an oddly breathless tone, came partly out of genuine curiosity and partly from the need to combat the strange languor stealing through her limbs in a brief silence during which Vince's dark gaze seemed intrigued with the shadowy crevice between her breasts.

The faint quirk at the corner of his mouth made her wonder if he hadn't read *both* those motives, but his answer was strictly in reply to her question.

"Apparently the fado clubs enjoy a large clientele of native Lisboners. No doubt you've read of the origin of the music in the lowly dock areas of the city. Then the gypsy singer Maria Severa brought it to the attention of the world in the last century. According to tradition, the contemporary female fadoists wear a black shawl in her memory."

Soon after that, they were shown to their table in the dining room and devoted themselves to a prolonged discussion of the menu. Finally they made their choices, agreeing to sample each other's food.

Alex ordered *sopa a alentejana*, a soup all the guidebooks insisted was a great favorite with the Portuguese. When it arrived, she discovered it to be a somewhat unpalatable watery brew with the faint taste of olive oil and garlic and with sodden squares of bread floating on top.

"How is it?" Vince inquired after watching her take the first spoonful.

"Here, you try it," she evaded, pushing the bowl toward him and then adding noncommitally, "it's different."

He dipped his soup spoon into the thin broth and tasted it, making exaggerated smacking sounds. His dark eyes gleamed with teasing mockery as they met hers.

"You're right," he pronounced solemnly. "It's definitely *different*."

She couldn't hold back the laughter gurgling up in her throat and he immediately joined in her hilarity.

The remainder of the meal was equally relaxed and enjoyable, with frequent bursts of merriment like that first one. Vince had ordered a Portuguese national favorite, salted codfish, while Alex had chosen broiled grouper with potatoes and tiny mussels still in their shells. They agreed without much deliberation that her meal was more to their liking than his.

The bottle of white Colares, the same vintage as that she had enjoyed unreservedly the previous evening, was emptied in an amazingly short time, what with all the tasting of unknown dishes, and Vince ordered another.

Just as the waiter was clearing away the dinner dishes, four very soberly dressed gentlemen took their places on straight-backed chairs placed at either side of a small platform in the center of the dining room. With all the cheer of musicians at a funeral, they began to tune their instruments: two guitars and two violas.

Then without any introduction or preliminary fuss, the first fado singer stepped up on the small stage and began an impassioned song which members of the audience greeted with loud handclaps and calls of approval as though it were a great favorite.

The young woman was very dramatic in her gestures and facial expressions, striding about the stage and managing to convey great heights and depths of emotion. The main themes of fado music, as Alex and Vince had discussed earlier over dinner, were betrayed or unrequited love, and the plaintive melodies were evocative of those emotions even to listeners who could not understand the Portuguese lyrics.

At one point in the evening, when the main star, Lucilio do Carmo, came on stage and translated into English a popular number she would sing, Alex had a moment of discomfort, wondering if Vince too was thinking of the parallel between the lyrics and their own relationship seven years ago. If so, he gave no visible sign, and she quickly shoved aside the momentary embarrassment.

Wine had never gone down so smoothly or disappeared so magically from her glass. By the time the second show had begun, Alex was clapping as enthusiastically as the true fado aficionado. Somehow her chair and Vince's had edged closer together so that his thigh pressed warmly against hers and his face was so near she could have sipped from his glass as easily as from her own.

In her state of euphoria, she could have stayed there

all night, content to remain in that drugging proximity with Vince. But when he asked if she was ready to go, she didn't demur but allowed him to lead her out to the taxi waiting on the street, one arm firmly around her waist.

Sometime between dinner and their departure from the club, she had answered rather explicitly the question her inner voice had posed that afternoon: *what do you want from Vince*? She knew now without any doubt she wanted him to be her lover. Just because she had no intentions of every remarrying, there was no reason she, a mature woman, should deny herself the pleasure of a mutually satisfying relationship with a mature man, and Vince was certainly that.

The only problem remaining in her mind was how to communicate her willingness to Vince if it wasn't clear already after the obvious care she had taken in dressing to attract him tonight and then her responsiveness during the evening. Fate in the guise of the taxi driver taking them back to the hotel seemed to be her coconspirator. He took curves at such speed that Alex felt herself sliding helplessly toward Vince.

"He must be training for the Grand Prix," Vince chuckled, pulling her close against him.

She melted unresistingly into his hard contours, slipping her arms around his waist with a contented little sigh and submitting her curvaceous softness to his male length. Once she felt his lips pressed gently against her hair and shivered with a spasm of pleasure. She could feel his heart pounding against her breasts when the taxi screeched to a halt outside the hotel, and when she stepped unsteadily out on the pavement, it was with the conviction that the termination of that wonderfully close embrace was a temporary one. Very soon she would feel his arms around her again—in either her room or his.

When he opened the door of the elevator for her to enter, she started to move past him and then stopped abruptly as she heard his words.

"Goodnight, Alex. I think I'll have a nightcap in the bar before I turn in."

She stared dumbly at the large old-fashioned key he dangled toward her and then looked up uncomprehendingly into his face, now an inscrutable mask. Then the reality finally sank in—he was rejecting what to her was a blatant invitation to come up to her room and make love to her. Disappointment, mortification, and then pride flashed across her expressive features.

"Goodnight, Vince," she managed, past lips stiffened to hide the tremor of hurt and took the key from his hand, taking care not to touch him. It seemed eons before he closed the door, leaving her alone with her overwhelming sensation of shame.

Chapter Four

ALEX'S FIRST THOUGHT upon awakening was that it seemed later than seven-thirty, the time she had requested breakfast to be served in her room. She had not asked for a wake-up telephone call, judging it to be unnecessary.

Then memory flooded back, bringing with it all the hurt, humiliation, and puzzlement that had made sleep so elusive last night. She relived that parting scene at the elevator and groaned aloud with shame. How *transparent* she must have been! How naïve he must think her! When she faced Vince this morning, how could she force herself to act natural, as if nothing had happened to disrupt the easy harmony of their relationship? And, even more disturbing to consider, how would he act toward her now? Would he be embarrassed? Patronizing? Pitying?

Getting out of bed and moving aside the heavy outer

47

draperies covering the glass doors to the balcony, she pondered the biggest enigma of all—*why* had Vince rejected her as he had? Without being conceited, she knew she was attractive enough to interest most men in Vince's situation. Was the answer that, in spite of all his assurances to the contrary, he *did* hold a grudge against her after all these years? Had he gained some sadistic pleasure from her own shame of rejection since she had spurned his love when she was eighteen? She simply could not accept the most obvious explanation—that he was not attracted to her physically. Her woman's intuition told her differently.

The brilliance and warmth of the sunshine flooding the room reinforced her earlier instincts about the lateness of the hour. She picked up her small gold watch from the top of the chest of drawers and gasped at the position of the hands.

Ten-thirty! That just *couldn't* be the correct time, she thought bewilderedly. And then something on the floor just inside the door caught her attention, and she walked over to pick up the sheet of paper, her movements slow with dread.

Canceled your breakfast order. Sleep late. You deserve it after the long hours yesterday. There was no salutation, no signature to the brief note which had, of course, to be from Vince.

The weakness in Alex's knees was the result of relief. She padded in her bare feet to the bed and sank down on the edge, not taking her eyes from that assertively male handwriting. After reading the message through more times than she could keep count of, she still could not discern the faintest undertone of censure or punishment. Finally, she could only conclude he had acted out of the same considerateness that had prompted him to order breakfast in her room the previous morning. Knowing that it had been well after midnight when they left th O'Faia Club, he had generously decided to allow her the extra sleep she badly needed.

What a nice human being he was!

The enigma of his actions last night still wasn't explained, but somehow Alex's anxieties were dissipated. The note had the same soothing effect on her that his physical presence did, instilling confidence and trust. On impulse, she picked up the telephone.

"Would you ring Mr. Reardon's room, please," she asked the receptionist.

"Mr. Reardon is not now in his room," came the precisely accented reply. "He expects to return at one o'clock, mademoiselle."

"Thank you." She couldn't curb the note of disappointment.

As soon as the receiver was replaced in the plain black cradle, she was startled by the telephone's abrasive ring. She picked up the receiver again.

"Yes?"

"Mademoiselle. Mr. Reardon left instructions that you would desire breakfast in your room when you awoke." His assertive words formed a statement, not a question, yet the ponderous silence seemed to require an answer.

"Why, yes. I would like breakfast now. Thank you very much."

Her inner glow of pleasure rivaled the brightness of the sunlight that streamed across the room and bathed her in warmth. Stretching luxuriously like a cat awakening from a nap on the hearth, she contemplated having breakfast on her own balcony and afterward writing some notes to people back home. How far away they seemed to her now, and how remote was that other life and former self. The problems and concerns so pressing just days ago were like shadowy memories to her now.

A couple of hours later, she had just finished a letter to Jinx when she looked up from her chair on the balcony and spied a familiar tall figure striding around a corner into view. Her pulse quickened in the pleasure of watching him as he moved along with the athletic grace of someone in peak physical condition.

He stopped short and gave her a warm smile of greeting. She stood up, went over to lean on the iron railing, and looked down at him. "You shouldn't have let me sleep half the day!" she called down to him in a chiding voice. "But I loved it!"

"Hungry?"

She wasn't surprised at his evasion of her oblique expression of gratitude for his thoughtfulness. "A little. Shall I meet you in the lobby?"

He glanced at his watch. "In twenty minutes."

"Aye-aye, sir."

The first hour or two in his company that afternoon, Alex was closely on guard for any slight indication of change in Vince's manner toward her. But there was none. Not a trace of contempt or triumph in his dark eyes, no comment or gesture to indicate any lowering of his regard for her.

After a while she could only conclude that her interpretation of their parting on the previous evening must have been distorted or at the least grossly exaggerated by her own imagination. What to her had seemed an abandoned response at the club and later in the taxi must not have appeared so to him. After all, she had married at eighteen and remained faithful to her husband since then. In actuality she was highly inexperienced in the intricacies of a courting relationship between a man and woman past the adolescent dating stage.

During the remainder of the week, she moved the whole matter into the recesses of her mind, having little time or energy to concern herself with anything but the engrossing work in which she was involved. For work it was, however enjoyable.

She and Vince visited tourist attractions, inspected shopping facilities, lunched and dined at various cafes and restaurants, investigated hotel accommodations and discussed package rates with the owners or managers, compiled detailed information on bus and metro schedules and prices, even attended a bullfight, which in Por-

tugal is different from those in Spain because the bull
is not killed.

Working daily with Vince refuted the old maxim
"familiarity breeds contempt," for with every passing
day her respect for him grew along with her admiration
as she observed firsthand evidence of his quick intelli-
gence coupled with a talent for communicating with people of all types. How could she have been so blind seven
years ago not to recognize all his good qualities? As
pointless as the reflection was, it recurred frequently.

She couldn't prevent herself from reflecting what a
wonderful husband he would have made—would *still*
make!—and the most timid of hopes was born. The two
of them were undeniably compatible working partners.
Might not that companionable relationship develop into
something deeper? *She* was certainly willing.

Then a small incident occurred to bring her sharply
back to reality. On Saturday they checked out of the
Hotel Jorge and took a taxi to the Cais de Sodre station
from which electric trains departed at frequent intervals
for nearby Estoril and Cascais. They had hotel reservations in Cascais and from there would explore the resort
town of Estoril, with its popular beach and gambling
casino. Then they would venture some miles farther to
the north to the picturesque mountain village of Sintra,
made famous by Lord Byron in his autobiographical
poem "Childe Harolde."

Sitting opposite them on the train was a shy young
Portuguese woman with a robust little boy who looked
about three years old. His eyes, so like his mother's,
were round and black and at first reflected an unwilling-
ness to respond to the strangers' smiles and friendly
overtures. Very soon, however, his diffidence in their
presence wore off and he proved himself a handful to his
mother, pulling and tugging to get free of her so that he
might roam at will through the railroad car. Her distress
was apparent as she struggled to subdue his willfulness.

Vince reached under the seat for his briefcase and

took out a catalog with full-color illustrations. In no time at all the small boy's attention was attracted, and then he was sitting on Vince's lap totally absorbed in turning the pages with his chubby fingers and pointing at what caught his fancy.

Alex watched with a stricken expression as the entranced child exclaimed in Portuguese and then looked up into Vince's face with a smile so enchanting it could have melted the coldest heart. Despair welled up inside her at the recollection of what she had grasped that first night in Lisbon and since then had either forgotten or pushed to the back of her consciousness—Vince wanted children of his own.

He had even implied that the only reason for marrying a woman was to father offspring. And even if her relationship with him *were* to develop into something deeper, it was unlikely *she* could ever give him children. In spite of the doctors' inability to prove her sterile, the fact remained that she had not been able to conceive during seven years of marriage. And Courtney, in one of his more savage moods, had assured her he had tangible evidence of *his* ability to father a child.

It was a relief when the young mother and the child left the train. Alex stared blindly out the window, almost totally oblivious to the lovely stretches of rocky coastline and the sparkle of the blue sea, the charming little villages with magenta bougainvillaea rambling along the walls of the houses and tiny front yards spilling over with brilliant blossoms.

"What's wrong?" Vince asked quietly.

She considered briefly trying to evade the question and dismissed the possibility of fooling him. He was much too perceptive about people, and she wasn't that accomplished an actress. Besides, deep down she had the desire to communicate to him the desolation she felt.

"There are certain times when I feel like an awful failure. Especially like today, when I see a mother and her child..." She found the going extremely difficult as her throat constricted and made the words sound hoarse and strained.

Vince looked down at her anguished face so searchingly she could imagine the intense gaze probing the depths of her soul and finding the answer for himself. "You have to forget Courtney, forget the past, Alex, if you're going to be truly free, which seems to be of paramount importance to you at this time."

He appeared to regret the terse words as soon as they were spoken. He lapsed into silence as if contemplating his own thoughts which, judging from the bleakness of his expression, were not very cheerful ones.

Alex pondered his words and realized she must not have revealed to him that first night in Lisbon, when she talked at length of the failure of her marriage, the total lack of real love between herself and Courtney. While she had no way of determining if Courtney had ever loved her with any depth, she knew he did not now, and her own infatuation for him had eroded steadily when she failed to detect the kind of worthwhile qualities that might have engendered a true, lasting love.

Evidently Vince had interpreted her depression today as stemming from regret over the breakup of her marriage. Perhaps it was better that he think that, better that he not know the truth—that *he*, not her former husband, was the cause of her sadness.

Minutes later the train slid to a halt in the Cascais station, and in the excitement of disembarking on a new adventure, Alex's somber mood quickly lifted. By some egalitarian stroke of good fortune, the Hotel Baia, though moderately priced, occupied the choice location in the whole village—overlooking the bay, or *baia*, and farther out the mighty Atlantic Ocean.

The hotel itself, an unpretentious rectangular building of terra-cotta brick, had four stories and a sun roof. All the rooms facing the harbor had private balconies furnished with a small round table of comfortable height for dining and two chairs.

A young bellboy rode up to the third floor with Alex
and Vince and opened her door with a flourish. Alex
went immediately to the wall opposite the door and
pushed aside heavy red draperies, which made the room
dim. What met her eyes was so enchanting she exclaimed
impulsively, "Oh, Vince. *Look* at this *view*!"

He came over and stood beside her and whistled
softly. "It's easy to see why this village is a great favorite
with artists and photographers." He pushed open the
heavy plate-glass door and followed her out onto the
balcony.

The scene they gazed down upon was one in which
vibrant color and perpetual movement combined so har-
moniously with the majesty of nature that one could
probably never tire of looking at it. A dozen or so fishing
boats lay at anchor out in the middle of the protected
bay, while scores of smaller rowboats dotted the spar-
kling blue surface of the water. All of the boats, both
large and small, were painted bright, glowing colors—
red, blue, green, yellow, and orange—and they formed
a kaleidoscope of graceful motion, swaying in unison to
the caprices of the breeze like dancers following in slow
motion the well-rehearsed movements of a dance.

Directly in front and to the right of the hotel was a
sand beach the same rich tawny color as Alex's hair. The
activity down there was fascinating, juxtaposing as it did
the old and the new: plain hard work and indolent leisure.
Several brightly painted fishing boats like those anchored
farther out leaned on their sides on the sand while men
in the drab blousy dress of fishermen worked busily
making repairs and applying new paint. Just yards away
from the working men were teenage girls sunbathing in
brief bikinis, small children scampering in the shallow
water and chasing beach balls, and farther down the
beach, a group of young males playing soccer with casual
skill.

To the left of the beach was a broad concrete quay
some thirty yards deep and extending to the farthest curve

of the bay. Scattered along the quay was an assortment of lean-to structures all boarded up now. Along the curb of the street and on the edge of the quay were vans and delapidated old cars from which spilled various wares sold by venders: colorful woven tablecloths, bulky woolen sweaters in drab colors, sea shells, and numerous other items, mostly manufactured, calculated to attract the eye of the souvenir-conscious tourist.

Alex couldn't tear herself away from the scene. Even with the constant movement and the noise of traffic down on the street, there was a beauty of form, a serenity that satisfied something deep inside her. She remained on the balcony while Vince responded to the polite prompting of the bellboy, who had been momentarily forgotten in the background. She was only dimly aware of Vince's voice as he spoke a few words of instructions, the boy's words of thanks for the tip he received, the quiet closing of the door.

When Vince came to stand behind her in the open doorway, she turned her head and smiled without any trace of self-consciousness, extending a hand welcoming him to rejoin her. After the briefest hesitation, he took the hand in his and stepped out on the balcony beside her, a little smile playing at the corners of his mouth as he read the rapt expression on her face.

"Lisbon was interesting and beautiful, but I *love* this . . ." With her free hand she made a graceful comprehensive gesture. And then shifting from the sublime to the practical, she asked, "How do those fishermen get the boats up on the sand like that? Do they pull them?" As far as she could determine, there were no mechanical aids such as a crane or marine railroad to hoist the boats up out of the water.

"By the oldest method in marine haul-outs—the same way their fathers and grandfathers before them did. At high tide they bring the boat into shore and anchor it in the sand. When the tide goes out again, the boat is left high and dry on the beach."

"How utterly *simple*—and ingenious!" Alex exclaimed, recalling how each year Courtney's father paid dearly to have his big yacht lifted out of the water, the bottom cleaned and painted with antifouling paint at a boatyard that had the latest in marine equipment. The romantic in her much preferred what she saw down there on the beach, the fishermen with trousers rolled up to their knees, attending personally to the wooden vessels that were their livelihood and obviously their pride as well. That care was given to appearance was evident in the jaunty contrasting stripes on the glossy hulls and in the names inscribed with painstaking neatness and individual flair.

After some minutes had passed, during which she sated her curiosity by firing one question after another at Vince, he turned back to the room, reminding her of mundane tasks such as unpacking which still had to be attended to. The sight of his luggage side by side with hers in the entranceway was evidence of what up to now she had been too swept away by her enthusiasm in the scenery to realize—Vince had dismissed the bellboy before he had the opportunity to see his own room.

"I hope your view is as spectacular as mine," she declared, watching him pick up his brown leather bag, which looked well worn beside her own smooth cream-colored leather suitcase.

He gave her an enigmatic half smile. "I only hope my neighbors don't keep me up all night with wild parties."

Titillated by that comment and by the teasing insinuation in his tone and manner, Alex followed him out into the corridor and watched as he fitted a key into the lock of the room next to hers. Realizing the proximity of their sleeping quarters aroused a distinct wave of pleasure, which she sought to conceal from him with a light retort.

"The walls of these older hotels *are* thin," she drawled. "I only hope *my* next-door neighbors don't snore." The quip calculated to produce a smile or a chuckle of amusement provoked a reaction so unexpected that it stopped her heart momentarily and then set it working again at triple time. As she spoke, Vince had been about to enter his room. He stopped in mid-stride and looked at her over his shoulder.

"Do *you* snore in your sleep, lovely Alex?" he asked softly, his dark eyes penetrating hers with devastating intensity. The tone of voice, one a lover might use in the midst of making love, raised prickles of awareness all along the surface of her skin, and she felt herself blushing like a teenager at the evocation of an image of tantalizing intimacy—Vince lying in bed alongside her, his dark hair rumpled on the pillow, his rugged face relaxed and vulnerable in sleep.

"You—you'd have to ask Courtney that," she blurted out without thinking. She immediately regretted having mentioned the name of her former husband as Vince stiffened visibly before her eyes and retreated behind the barrier of casual reserve he maintained between them.

"We'll have to work out a set of signals—two taps on the wall means turn down the radio and so on," he joked. "See you in a little while."

With these words he entered his room and closed the door behind him, leaving Alex standing in the corridor despising herself for having been such a fool. The first sign that Vince might have a flicker of interest in her as a woman and not just as a working associate and she managed to say the precise words to erect the wall of the past between them again. Seething with self-contempt, she went back into her room and set about unpacking, the whole time straining her ears for sounds from the room next-door.

At dusk, the focus of activity down at the harbor shifted from the beach to the concrete quay. The sunbathers departed, only a persistent few remaining, mostly loud young men tirelessly engaged in a vigorous game of soccer which included water as well as sand in its field of play. A few fishermen sold fresh sardines from rowboats pulled up on the sand, the buyers mostly middle-aged women who came away with a few fish glinting like burnished aluminum through clear plastic bags.

Alex and Vince wandered to the end of the quay farthest from the sand beach and watched the unloading of the day's fishing catch. The bay was crowded with large fishing boats, at anchor now that the fleet was in, and small rowboats plied back and forth between them and the quay, delivering rectangular plastic boxes packed neatly with various kinds of fish. Men waiting on the quay took the boxes handed up to them from the rowboats and carried them off down a narrow alley, presumably to some refrigerated warehouse or fish market.

As darkness fell over the bay, the lights along the quay assumed a dazzling brightness. It contributed to the carnival atmosphere unfolding with incredible swiftness, like a night-blooming flower, as one by one the fronts of the motley collection of small lean-tos Alex had noticed earlier were opened and their function as booths became apparent. Some of them lured passersby to play betting games while others offered various kinds of food and drink and still others trinkets.

The aroma of grilling sardines pervaded the entire quay as portable braziers were fired up. Music blared from speakers overhead, a bizarrely incongruous assortment of rhythms ranging from old Chuck Berry rock-and-roll favorites to plaintive fado ballads. And from every direction came groups of people of all ages, laughing and talking with boisterous good humor.

Alex could only hope for a multitude, for the jostling of the crowd soon brought the firm clasp of Vince's hand at her waist and then eventually the protective curve of his arm around her shoulder. Following her deepest instincts, she nestled closer to him as they wandered from one booth to another, staying on the outskirts and watching in some fascination the unrestrained manner in which people were enjoying themselves.

An adventurous impulse led them to join the patrons of a food booth much larger than all the rest, actually more of an open-air cafe with tables and benches. The fare was simple and limited: either sardines or chicken pieces cooked on open grills just outside the booth, roasted potatoes, a salad of fresh sliced tomatoes, rolls, and a choice of beer or soft drink. The food was served on plastic platters and the drinks in cans, with paper cups available for the more discriminating.

Alex was reminded of county fairs in rural Georgia, but the chicken there had been golden-fried in a batter. When she mentioned that whimsical association to Vince, he agreed to the unlikely similarity with a smile that warmed the very marrow of her bones. All her feminine instincts insisted there was a subtle difference tonight in his look, in his touch, an increased intimacy that was as much responsible for the golden luminosity of Alex's eyes and the lovely flush on her cheeks as the gala atmosphere surrounding them.

After the ample meal, they wandered back toward the end of the quay where the fish had been unloaded earlier. There, on a makeshift platform enclosed in a three-sided shelter, a rock band had begun to play and sing songs that were all originally recorded and made popular in the States. Alex found it intriguing to hear American slang reproduced with only the faintest accent by the young Portuguese musicians who perhaps didn't even know what they were singing.

After a while, though, she tired of the mounting din all around them and was delighted to hear Vince murmur in her ear, "Like to walk?" Without any discussion of destination, they skirted the crowd and headed in the general direction of the hotel. The street which ran in front of the hotel curved sharply following the contour of the bay toward the ocean, ascending a steep hill and then veering again, this time to the right, to run alongside the ocean.

They strolled slowly along the sidewalk and before

long found themselves blessedly out of hearing of the sounds of revelry as they came to the outskirts of the town. On the opposite side of the street were villas secluded behind high walls and dense shrubbery. To their immediate left just beyond the sidewalk pavement was rocky terrain and some yards beyond that the black infinity of the Atlantic Ocean. Far out in the darkness they could see brilliant pinpricks of light indicating the positions of ships at anchor.

Except for an occasional car driving past, they were alone with the hushed immensity of ocean and sky, the night air cool against their faces and sweetly scented with blossoms from the gardens of the villas. Walking arm in arm with Vince, Alex felt her heart swell with joy. It was one of those rare times when two people are in complete harmony and words are unnecessary.

After a while the villas were farther apart and the cars less frequent. Later Alex was unable to remember just how it happened that they no longer were walking but just standing side by side gazing out at the obsidian ocean, his arm around her waist and her arm around his waist underneath his jacket.

She leaned her head against his shoulder, closing her eyes and breathing a little sigh of exquisite contentment. The touch of his fingertips on her cheek was as light as the brush of a waxy rose petal, and she lifted her face in an instinctive gesture of supplication. The long fingers she so admired for their supple strength and sensitivity traced the curvature of her jawline, the outlines of her lips, which quivered to his touch, and followed every delicate plane and soft curve of her face unhurriedly, like the seeing hand of a blind man.

Transfixed, Alex held her breath as the light, tantalizing exploration dropped to the sensitive curve of her neck. Shivering, she turned toward him and waited for what seemed an unendurable span of time for the slow descent of his lips to hers. After a century or two, she felt his mouth cool and firm as she knew it would be, lacking any haste or urgency as he took little exploratory tastes of her lips.

Her hands slipped up over the firmness of his chest and pulled his head downward in an involuntary effort to satisfy the restless hunger he was arousing for a kiss of more passion and depth. Her gesture of impatience coupled with the imploring moan deep in her throat snapped his restraint, and his mouth moved on hers with devouring fierceness. Her lips parted and welcomed the ravaging of his tongue which sought and found hers.

His hands explored the pliant curves of her body, encountering no discouragement as they came up to cup the fullness of her breasts. Weak with the languor of desire coursing through her veins, Alex clung to him for support. Her chest was heaving with the difficulty of breathing when he finally tore his mouth from the bruised clinging softness of hers as though the act required of him a monumental effort.

His breath came in hot gusts against her sensitive flesh as he buried his face into the curve of her neck. Wrapping his arms around her hips, he gathered her up hard against him so that she could feel the thunderous beat of his heart, the convulsive shudder which shook his powerful frame, and the thrust of his maleness against her yielding feminine contours. It was obvious that he wanted her as much as she wanted him and the knowledge bubbled joyously through her veins.

"We'd better go back," he murmured huskily against her skin, and released her.

The inarticulate sound of protest she made felt as if it sprang from the vital core of her being, but once he had pulled apart from her with gentle finality, her reason returned. He was right, of course. They couldn't make love on the sidewalk or the rocky ground off to the side.

Without further resistance she walked beside him back toward the hotel, neither of them speaking. Alex assumed that he, like herself, was still held in the thrall of what had happened between them and was unwilling, as she was, to tarnish the magic with mere words. There was in her mind no regret concerning the past, no consideration of the future, and absolute certainty of what would happen when they arrived back at the hotel. How fortunate they were that there was no innocent person to be injured—no husband or wife in the picture. They were two adults having long since reached the age of consent, and she wanted more intensely than she had ever wanted anything in her life to break through that barrier separating her from him. She longed for the closeness with him that would assuage the throbbing ache deep inside her.

Preceding Vince into the lobby, she blinked irritably at the brightness of the lights and waited in front of one of the elevators as he claimed their keys from an eagerly obliging bellboy. Vince had reached the elevator and was about to open the door for her when the hall porter, who had been busy with a guest when they entered, called out Vince's name.

Alex glanced up and saw Vince's face clearly in the full light for the first time. A jagged shard of fear pierced her chest at the remote, utterly impassive expression on his face. If he felt the way she did, he couldn't possibly look like that, a voice of dismay cried out inside her.

She listened numbly, with a growing sense of dread, as the porter explained Vince had received numerous telephone calls during his absence, all from the same caller, who was urgently trying to contact him. "This person requests that you return the call no matter how late." He came from behind the counter and handed Vince a folded slip of paper.

Something in the man's bland expression and the oddly neutral wording clutched at Alex's chest with premonition, and she made no pretense of not looking at the slip of paper Vince held in his hand. The bold lettering in black ink was easy to decipher: *Gloria Allen*, and then the digits of a telephone number.

Vince studied it briefly, his expression unreadable.

Without comment, he stuffed the paper in a pocket of his jacket and opened the elevator door.

Disappointment was a heavy weight on Alex's chest as she stepped inside. She didn't need to wait until they arrived at their rooms, side by side on the third floor, to know what she had looked forward to with such anticipation and sureness on that silent walk back to the hotel was doomed not to happen. The interlude in the darkness near the ocean might have been a figment of her imagination for all the reality it possessed now. No residue of passion lingered in Vince's dark eyes or on the inscrutable mask of his features as he unlocked her door, removed the key, and handed it to her before stepping politely aside for her to enter.

Pride came to her rescue when she realized he was probably restraining his impatience to get to his own room and telephone that Gloria Allen female, whoever *she* was. The last thing Alex wanted was to let him see how hurt she was by his distant manner, how devastatingly disappointed at the smashing of her hopes . . .

"Goodnight, Vince." It was much to her credit that she got the words past the oversized obstruction in her throat and even managed a tight little smile. "I know you're anxious to call your woman friend." She was justly proud of herself for that airy little comment, considering the expenditure of effort it cost her. She wanted him to know she *had* seen that name on the slip of paper and wasn't in the *least* jealous.

For just a split second he looked blankly at her as if trying to fathom the content of her flippant words, and then his hand went to the pocket where he had placed the note.

"Goodnight, Alex. Sleep well." He might have been addressing a stranger passing by in the hallway for all the warmth the words contained.

Sleep well. The sheer nerve of him to tell her that, Alex raged as she shut the door behind her and leaned on it for support. She would be lucky to sleep at all considering the state of her nerves.

The brief spurt of fury died quickly and her body sagged despondently as she crossed the room and shut the heavy glass door on the loud music, the cacaphony of human voices and laughter drifting up from the quay. After she had pulled the heavy draperies, the noise was reduced to a muted level that served as an accompaniment to her restless pacing and tormented thoughts.

What a fool she was to be jealous of this unknown woman in Vince's life. It should come as no surprise that a man as vital and attractive as Vince had female friends. But she must *not* jump to conclusions. Vince hadn't once mentioned Gloria Allen or given Alex any reason to believe he had someone special in his life. If he had, wouldn't he have made at least casual mention of her?

What she knew with irrefutable certainty was that Vince had been as aroused as she was tonight, had wanted and needed her as much as she wanted and needed him. Therefore, what she *should* do, if she possessed half an ounce of courage, was go to his room, knock on the door, and ask him point-blank what had made him draw back from her as he had.

She could come up with only two possibilities to explain his behavior. The first was pride. Perhaps he wanted her to retract that clumsy *keep-off* restriction she had so tactlessly established their first night in Lisbon. Or maybe he didn't want to become involved in an affair with her for fear she might have expectations of permanency he was unwilling to fulfill.

It would take only a minute for her to sweep aside both reservations, and she desperately wished she had the nerve to take those few steps to his door.... But what if Gloria Allen *was* someone important, someone with a claim to his fidelity?

That chilling possibility sapped Alex's courage. Finally, she admitted to herself her cowardice and prepared for bed, taking a long soak in the tub in the futile hope that it would relax her bunched muscles and allow her to fall asleep.

An hour later she was still trying to find a comfortable position in the narrow bed, flopping on her back, turning to curl on one side and then the other. It seemed as if she would never get to sleep. A slight sound arrested her attention and she concentrated all her powers on listening. There it was again, coming from Vince's room next-door. He must be unable to sleep too.

For some inexplicable reason that knowledge had a benign, soothing effect on Alex. Minutes later she was asleep.

Chapter Five

HALF ASLEEP, ALEX responded to the insistent knocking
on her door, too groggy to have the presence of mind
to put on a robe over the insubstantial lace and silk of
her nightgown. What she saw when she had coped fum-
blingly with the lock and opened the door wide enough
to peer outside so took her by surprise that she swung
the door wide and blinked in astonishment. Vince stood
there holding a heavily laden tray which even in her
torpor she realized was breakfast.

"Your balcony or mine?" he inquired with eyebrows
raised humorously and a broad smile warmly indulgent
of her sleepiness. His darkly intent gaze roved over the
rumpled honey-gold of her hair and then slid lower, reminding her suddenly of how little the scanty nightgown
actually concealed.

Shy and flustered in a way she knew was ridiculous

for a woman who had shared a bedroom with a man for seven years, Alex edged back until she was partially hidden behind the door. She motioned him to enter and he did so, passing so close beside her that her senses were assailed with the impact of his masculinity and a smile of simple delight at his presence made her curve her lips in a smile. The core of warmth born inside her at the first glimpse of him outside her room radiated pleasure and well-being to the furthest extremities of her limbs, awakening every sluggish cell and nerve end in her body until the last trace of sleepiness had vanished and she felt vibrantly alive.

Held in the grip of a strange paralysis, she watched his sure movements. He set the tray down on the combination desk-dresser, swept aside the crimson draperies and opened the glass door, propping it with a brick put there for that purpose. When he turned back into the room to retrieve the tray, a quick appraisal from those dark eyes, like a fiery caress over her sensitized flesh, produced an energizing effect and she fled to the bathroom.

The robe matching her nightgown, both champagne silk and trimmed lavishly in cobwebby lace, hung on a hook behind the bathroom door. She donned the covering immediately, as though Vince's eyes could penetrate the plaster walls. The robe was actually an imposture if its purpose was to conceal the bewitching curves of her figure, but she could hardly take the time to dress fully when Vince was waiting for her with breakfast out on the balcony. After splashing cold water on her face and pulling a brush quickly through her hair, she went out to join him.

Sitting in the chair opposite him, she watched the steady ease of his hands as he poured her a cup of coffee and diluted it liberally with boiled milk. *Last night those same hands had caressed her face with devastating gentleness, had explored the intimate curves of her body...*

"Sugar?" His dark eyes interrogated hers, thrilling her with the awareness in their depths.

"No, thanks." She accepted the cup from him and took a sip. "You're spoiling me unmercifully. Aren't you afraid I'll come to expect this kind of pampering?"

"What man could refuse you anything in that outfit you're wearing?" The husky lightness of the words was belied by the burning intensity of his eyes as they rested on the deep neckline of the robe, where it more than suggested the swell of her breasts.

Her heart pumped a loud response that made the blood thud against her eardrums. But Vince quickly directed the conversation into impersonal channels by calling attention to the disappearance of all but one of the fishing boats they had observed being repaired on the beach yesterday. The elation coursing through Alex's veins gradually subsided.

Breaking open a roll, she spread it with rich butter that had a grainier consistency than that to which she was accustomed and added a generous layer of tart marmalade. The food might have been ambrosia of the gods it tasted so delicious and she herself a member of the illustrious Olympian assembly looking down contentedly on a world of mere humans. As all the pores of her skin opened to the languorous warmth of the sunshine bathing the balcony, once more the recesses of her mind were swept clean of last night's doubts and distresses by a pure joy of well-being as all her senses surrendered to the captivating beauty of the morning. At that moment she could have thought of nothing to add to her happiness, except the promise of many more mornings like this one in enchanting surroundings... *with Vince*.

Their appetites eventually sated, the conversation grew so desultory that Alex could feel drowsiness weighting her eyelids. They flew open when Vince scraped back his chair and stood up.

"Wake up, lazybones. You have thirty minutes to get yourself dressed while I make a few telephone calls."

The mention of telephone calls was a dash of ice-cold water in Alex's sun-warmed face, reminding her of what she had completely forgotten or pushed to a dim corner of her mind—Gloria Allen. Was *she* one of the calls he had to make? Had he been unable to contact her last night? Had he even tried?

These questions chased around the corners of her mind as she dressed, following Vince's example and donning jeans that hugged her slim hips and long shapely legs. Mindful of the summer warmth of the sun beaming down onto the balcony, she pulled on a sleeveless knit top designed so that it didn't quite meet the waistband of her jeans, leaving a narrow but provocative band of exposed midriff.

Considering the casualness of her dress, she applied the minimum of make-up, a touch of lip gloss, and left the room after a cursory inspection of herself in the mirror. She didn't look a lot older than she had when she first met Vince so long ago.

His door was slightly ajar, and her tentative knock brought a decisive "Come in" from inside the room. He was talking on the telephone, and she hesitated just beyond the foyer until he looked up and saw her, gesturing for her to come in. She thrust her hands into the pockets of her jeans and sauntered over to look out at the view identical to her own, keenly aware of his gaze following her.

He was sitting on the edge of the twin bed he had not slept in and balanced a notepad on his knee. In the form-fitting jeans and short-sleeved knit shirt that hugged his muscular shoulders, he looked disturbingly vital and masculine, not at all like the high-powered executive she knew he was. His part of the conversation, which was readily identifiable as Globe Travel business, was crisp and authoritative.

Submitting to an irrepressible curiosity, Alex turned back toward the room and looked around as though she hoped to find some as yet undiscovered key to his per-

sonality. The arrangement of his possessions had a casual
order indicative of one who is impatient of time wasted
in unnecessary searching for a needed article and yet is
not rigidly fastidious. The furnishings of the room were
identical to hers, yet the impact of his own personality
made the atmosphere clearly masculine.

Suddenly she was aware that he no longer was talking
on the telephone and was regarding her with marked
amusement. "Well? Do I rate at least a cee-minus on
neatness?"

She pretended to deliberate, hoping the real nature of
her scrutiny of his private quarters was not transparent
to him. "Definitely a cee-minus at the very least," she
pronounced with a thoughtful nod. Then ingenuousness
surfaced in a sheepish admission. "Actually you're much
neater than I am."

He stood up, seeming taller than ever in the small
room. His smile was enigmatic as he commented, "Your
room reflects your personality and intense femininity."

Alex couldn't have been more stunned if he had just
inventoried the contents of her handbag. He hadn't even
seemed to *look* at her room. She would have loved to
pursue the subject of just how he perceived her personality and whether the "intense femininity" with which he
attributed her was an admirable trait.

But it was immediately apparent that the cryptic ob-
servation was the beginning and end of the conversation.
By now she was becoming accustomed to the lightning
changes of his moods and the consummate facility with
which he bridged the transition from one to another.
Whenever a subject posed hazardous depths he chose not
to explore further, he stepped nimbly to safer ground as
he did now, consulting his wristwatch and suggesting
they be on their way.

The small shops in Cascais offered a fascination all
their own, and Alex soon became absorbed in the purchase of small gifts to take back to her family and special
friends. Vince seemingly possessed a bottomless fund

of patience, never once betraying restlessness as she agonized over the relative merits of each selection. Once, looking up to catch him watching her with telltale amusement, she explained ruefully, "I can't help it. I'm a Pisces, and I can *never* seem to make up my mind." Picking up the two brightly painted pieces of pottery she had been deliberating over, she held them out toward him. "Which one of these would *you* buy?" she asked impulsively.

"That one." He pointed to his choice without a second's hesitation.

"I'll *take* that one," she told the salesgirl and then smiled up at him as they waited for the purchase to be wrapped. "Don't *you* ever have trouble making up your mind what you want?"

For a moment she thought she must have blundered up against another conversational impasse and that he was going to ignore her question.

"My problem in decision-making is precisely the opposite of yours," he said finally. "I know immediately what I want."

"But that's not a problem!" she objected.

"Isn't it?" The expression in the dark eyes was unfathomable to her, and when he spoke again, she knew the conversation had been changed.

The pottery saucer was the last memento she would buy to take home to Georgia, but on the way back to the hotel for lunch, Alex paused in front of a boutique to admire a colorful display of bikinis. In her mind was the unspoken longing for a new swimsuit to wear on the beach in Estoril that afternoon.

She looked up at Vince, parted her lips to ask if they could spare the time for her to select a swimsuit, and then closed them at the determined expression on his face. "On one condition," he replied in answer to her unspoken question. "*I* get to pick it out."

In an amazingly short time they emerged from the boutique with her new bikini, undoubtedly the most dar-

ing one she had ever possessed, its boldly diagonal purple
and white stripes seeming to emphasize the brevity of
the material.

"Maybe that's what I need," she suggested recklessly.
"Someone to make up my mind for me." And when that
provocative comment bounced off the impenetrable wall
of his silence, she retreated quickly behind a smokescreen
of flippancy. "On second thought, that sounds too much
like a husband."

The Hotel Baia was a popular lunch spot because of
its advantageous location. The plaza in front of the hotel
was crowded to capacity with small round tables shaded
by colorful umbrellas and more likely than not, one had
to wait a few minutes for a vacant table.

By this time Alex's zeal for eating native fare had
been tempered somewhat, and she was able to select
foods lacking an aura of strangeness without being overwhelmed with guilt. Today she ordered a shrimp salad
that proved to be delicious and completely familiar in its
appearance and ingredients.

After lunch they walked several blocks to the small,
dingy train station, the front of which also served as a
major bus stop, and boarded a bus for Estoril. In American money, the cost of the tickets was less than a dime
apiece.

A few minutes later they climbed down from the bus
across the street from the Parque Estoril, a huge beautifully landscaped garden roughly the size of a football
field. Alex gazed longingly across at it, and taking in her
expression, Vince asked if she would like to stroll
through the park before they went to the beach, which
was located in the opposite direction.

They walked all the way to the casino, a building of
all modern planes and plate glass rising behind the park.
It seemed deserted this early in the day, and no one
appeared to order them off the premises when they
mounted the steps to a large balcony fronting the entire

second story. From that vantage the view was a panorama of vivid colors—the verdant green of the park forming a background for the brilliant reds, purples, and yellows of the luxuriant blossoms in the formally planted beds. And beyond the busy highway separating the park from the golden sand of the beach extended the azure ocean. Over the whole was a pale blue sky devoid of a single cloud.

Gazing out of it, Alex wondered if one could ever become glutted on beauty. It seemed there was no end to the magnificence of scenery offered by this small country.

A few minutes later they had retraced their steps, crossed over the highway, and entered an underground tunnel which gave access to the beach. Coming out again into the brilliant sunlight, Alex gazed around her and felt utterly amazed.

She already knew that the sand along this coast was not snowy white as was the sand to which she was accustomed in Georgia and Florida. It was the warm tawny color of the rock from which it was formed. But what met her fascinated gaze along the beach was unlike anything she had ever seen in the States.

It seemed that every square inch of sand was occupied by human beings, and not in any haphazard manner either. The beach was divided by posts into rectangular portions so that each small party had its own prescribed territory. A great number of the rectangular areas were shaded by awnings attached to the tops of the posts.

Walking beside Vince farther down the beach to their left, Alex soon realized that the beach was almost a complete world in itself, where one could come for the day and have all needs taken care of. It was possible to rent everything from canvas awnings to deck chairs to beach towels. There were beach houses where one could pay a small sum for a shower, a hot one costing slightly more than a cold one! Food and drink were available at premium prices at a large open-fronted restaurant, but many people brought their own wicker lunch hampers and coolers of drinks. Those who preferred to swim in a swimming pool could pay whole or half-day rates to use one of several public pools built up on a terrace so that they overlooked the sand and ocean below.

After exploring all the facilities available on the densely populated section of the beach, they decided to seek out a more secluded spot, which they found after walking some distance. There they spread their beach towels on the sand. From here they could look straight across the expanse of blue ocean and see the Bay of Cascais. The Hotel Baia was a tiny Monopoly-size hotel and the fishing boats mere dots of color.

The time came for Alex to remove her jeans and top and reveal the brevity of the bikini she had purchased earlier in the day. She was grateful that, aside from an appreciative sweeping survey, Vince made no fuss over the generous spilling of her curves from the minute pieces of the swimsuit of his choice.

She was the one guilty of staring when he stripped down to abbreviated black nylon trunks that hugged very low on his hips and left no doubt of his maleness. She was disconcertingly aware of him as he stretched out beside her on his own towel, his skin noticeably dark in contrast to hers. He obviously spent a lot of time in the sun, probably year-round, as his work would allow him to do.

Fortunately he lay with his eyes closed, so she could look to her contentment at the tautness of the muscles in his shoulders and back, the trim narrowness of his waist, the long, powerfully built legs. The palms of her hands itched at the thought of stroking the firm elasticity of the skin covering those smooth ridges in his back. She could imagine without any difficulty the quiver of his flesh coming to life under her hand.

He swung to his feet with a suddenness that made her flinch guiltily, as if she had actually enacted her fantasy. "Ready to try the water?" he asked.

Rising, she took his proffered hand and ran beside him down to the water's edge and plunged in. The shock of icy coldness literally took her breath away and she tried vainly to pull back from the hand which dragged her in with him. Succumbing finally to the inevitable, she swam beside him, the vigor of her strokes alleviating to a small measure the numbness of her limbs.

Her teeth were still chattering a few minutes later when she left the frigid water and paced across the sand to her towel, reaching up to ring out the excess water from her hair.

"You *knew*!" she accused, laughing and turning to confront him when he came up behind her, water streaming down his lithe, muscular body.

"I knew," he admitted. His look of amusement died as he stared at her.

She glanced down at herself and then lowered her arms when she saw why he was staring at her. The thin silken fabric of her new bikini became semitransparent when it was wet, clinging like a second skin to her body and broadcasting the hardness of her nipples, which had leaped into prominence in protest of the icy onslaught of ocean water. To conceal her self-consciousness, she flopped face down on her towel.

In a short while she was completely relaxed again and thawed by the warmth of the sun. They sunbathed side by side, talking little. Several times Vince went back into the water, but he did not insist that Alex accompany him. Since that first time, an electric current of awareness vibrated in the air between them, undermining their several efforts at impersonal conversation.

Alex did not argue when Vince commented that she had probably had enough sun for one day. Rising from her towel, she pulled on her jeans and top over the vivid purple and white stripes which by now were completely dry.

After leaving the beach, they walked along the arcaded walkways lined with shops on either side of the Parque

Estoril, killing time before the next bus to Cascais arrived. The high prices and air of exclusivity about the boutiques signaled the wealth of those who made Estoril a fashionable resort. Personally, Alex preferred the humbler and more quaint atmosphere of Cascais.

By the time they boarded the bus, she had that pleasant tiredness that usually followed a day on the beach or out on the open water in a boat. The prospect of having to get dressed to go out to dinner didn't appeal to her at all, a fact which she mentioned to Vince only to discover he was thinking precisely the same thing.

"Why don't we just stop at a market on the way to the hotel and pick up something for dinner," she suggested, noticing that the afternoon in the sun had deepened the tan on his face.

"Good idea," he agreed.

They spent some time browsing in the small market they found less than a block from the hotel. What had initially been planned as a simple repast took on the dimensions of a feast as they selected bread, several kinds of cheese, fruit, and wine. At the hotel, they agreed to have supper on Vince's balcony as soon as they had both showered and changed. Lunch seemed a long time past now as hunger pangs rumbled in Alex's stomach.

She had a bath instead of a shower and almost fell asleep in the tub of fragrant suds. Drying herself off with a huge towel that apparently was typical of old-fashioned European hotels, she pondered what to wear. In her present state of comfortable fatigue, she would have liked to slip into her nightgown and robe, but that was clearly inappropriate under the circumstances. The next best choice was a pale green slacks outfit made of a soft synthetic fabric that had the texture of velvet. Its simple lines made it adaptable for almost any occasion while permitting her the freedom of doing without a bra.

Vince's hair was damp and slicked down against his head when he opened the door to admit her. He wore dark slacks which suggested the muscular power of his thighs and a maroon silk shirt which emphasized the darkness of his tanned skin.

"It just isn't fair!" she exclaimed to combat the effects of his darkly appreciative gaze. "You just get a darker tan while my nose looks like a beacon."

"I haven't gotten to your nose yet," he murmured as she swept past him.

The sight that met her on the balcony made her gasp in surprise and pleasure. "How elegant this looks!" The small table was draped with a linen tablecloth and set with stemmed wine glasses, white china with the hotel's emblem, and heavy silver cutlery.

He had been standing in front of the dresser opening a bottle of wine and brought it out to the balcony. She watched him fill the glasses, strongly conscious of the quiet assurance with which he did everything.

Then he pulled out her chair and seated her close to the table. "Hmm, you smell good enough to eat," he murmured and then took his own place, leaving her scalp tingling just under the spot where she could *swear* he had lightly placed his lips.

The wine, a red Dão with a colorful label, was smooth and light, a perfect accompaniment to the creamy pale cheese and hard rolls. They both ate with appetite, feeling no need to make idle conversation to fill up the comfortable silence. They did discuss briefly their plans to visit Sintra the following day, where they would tour two historic palaces.

Alex sighed with deep contentment as the light over the harbor mellowed, giving depth and resonance to the colors that were so brilliant in the glare of full sunshine. The tranquility and serene beauty of the scene before her touched a sensitive chord in her soul and aroused humble gratitude for the privilege she had to experience firsthand this kind of aesthetic pleasure.

Instinctively she glanced over at Vince, wanting to share with him her feelings and ascertain his own. The remoteness of his expression, indicating he had withdrawn somewhere deep within himself, made it impossible for her to speak or reach across the gulf of silence. What was he thinking to cause the tautness she perceived in his profile, to make him oblivious, as he seemed to be, of his surroundings and of her?

Dusk fell quickly, resurrecting the nighttime personality of the quay they had observed the previous evening. The booths were opened, loud music burst through the speakers as if pent up with energy after the day's rest, and people appeared out of nowhere. Alex wondered idly if the transformation was a weekend phenomenon or if it occurred on week nights too. From her perspective up above it all, she felt very detached and very content to be where she was. Vince had mentioned that they could go down there later, but at the moment she felt pleasantly tired and drowsy. A low chuckle from close by made her aware she was yawning.

"I hope it's not the company," he teased, his teeth very white in the dim light. And then he yawned himself, and they both broke into spontaneous laughter.

"What a couple of old fogeys," Alex giggled and then gave in to another cavernous yawn. "It must be the wine."

In spite of her efforts to clear the fuzziness from her brain, she found it impossible to keep her leaden eyelids from closing and several times was jerked to consciousness by the painful snapping of her neck as her head fell to one side. This had just happened once again and she was blinking in an effort to combat the terrible grogginess when Vince stood up with an impatient oath.

"We're sitting out here falling asleep in our chairs when there are two perfectly comfortable beds inside. We can catch a nap and then go out and sample some night life later if we're in the mood."

The impact of what he was suggesting, that she lie down on one of the twin beds in his room and go to sleep with him in the other one, increased the tempo of her heartbeat and brought her wide awake as she followed him into the darkened room. He kicked off his shoes and lay down with a loud sigh on one of the two narrow beds. Not knowing what else to do, she followed his example, even though she wasn't in the least sleepy now. It would look ridiculously priggish to insist upon returning to her own room, especially since the regularity of Vince's breathing indicated he must have fallen immediately asleep and harbored no erotic intentions.

Lying stretched out on her back, she listened to the sounds from the quay and reflected on the irony of her present position. Last night she had wanted desperately to muster the nerve to come to this very room and reveal honestly to Vince her desire that he make love to her. Now he lay relaxed and sound asleep just a few feet away, and they might just as well be separated by the wall between their bedrooms. Awareness of his physical closeness made sleep an impossibility, and after a while her back began to ache from the rigidity of her position. Trying not to make any noise, she eased over on one side so that she faced the open door to the balcony. In a few minutes her shoulder went numb and she turned to the other side, less cautious about her movements in the assumption that Vince was asleep and wouldn't hear her. No position was comfortable for longer than a minute or two.

"Stop worrying and go to sleep, Alex. You're perfectly safe here with me."

The low command stunned her, refuting as it did her assumption that Vince was asleep and totally oblivious to her restlessness. Had he been lying there listening to her sighs of exasperation? She didn't know whether to laugh or cry at the supreme irony of his assurance that she was "safe" with him. Without doubt being "safe" around him was the last thing she wanted—if her interpretation of his meaning was correct!

It wasn't just sexual fulfillment she longed for either, although that was undeniably a part of it. She wanted closeness with him. She wanted him to hold her tight in his arms so that his heartbeat drummed in time with hers, so that the warmth of his body penetrated her muscles and bones and flesh.

What she conjured in her imagination was so sweet and yet so elusive she felt the wetness of her lashes against her cheek. Wrapping her arms tightly around herself, she permitted her fantasies full rein and drifted off into a wonderful world of warmth and closeness . . .

Chapter Six

AT FIRST SHE didn't know where she was and couldn't identify the noises coming from the next room. The faint, diffused light that came through the drawn curtains shed a gray illumination over the furnishings of the room, which were familiar but not quite right in their placement. The twin beds should be against the opposite wall, shouldn't they? And then she saw that the other bed had been slept in and knew the truth at once. She was still in Vince's room!

The last thing she could remember about last night was being unable to fall asleep as she lay fully dressed *on top of the covers*. Now she was snuggled warmly under the sheet and bedspread, and she was... *naked*! Alex's hands slid over her body verifying the bareness of her flesh except for brief nylon panties, the only underwear she had worn under the slacks outfit last evening.

Her mind grappled with the astonishing deduction that some time during the night Vince must have undressed her and placed her beneath the covers without arousing her from sleep. *Unless*—a disconcerting possibility posed itself—unless there was some other explanation for her bare flesh. Could she have made love with him in a state of unconsciousness?

Of course not! What a ridiculous notion!

Now she identified those original puzzling sounds as the splash of water in the bathroom as it fell against the plastic shower curtain and the porcelain of the tub. Vince was taking a shower. Any minute now he would come back into the room and she would have to face him with this baffling gap in her memory.

Acting in a mindless surge of panic, she threw back the bed covers and dressed swiftly in her clothes, which lay neatly draped over the back of a chair. With her shoes and handbag gathered up into her arms, she fled the room noiselessly in her bare feet, giving no thought to what someone passing in the corridor might think after a cursory glance at her sleep-touseled hair and disheveled appearance, not to mention the clandestine manner of leave-taking.

Luck was in her favor, and she met no one before gaining the safety of her own room. Immediately she felt sheepish and embarrassed at the blind impulsiveness of her flight. As she pondered what she had done, she saw that her behavior was plainly contradictory. Hadn't she already admitted openly to herself a longing for physical intimacy with Vince? What could possibly be more promising of such intimacy than to be nearly naked in his bedroom while he showered in the adjoining bathroom with the door ajar as it had been?

With chagrin Alex realized she had panicked like a virginal maiden in an old-fashioned tale of romance, but it was too late now to go back and resume what might have evolved with total naturalness if she had remained. What was done was done, and the day held far too much promise for her to stand around and mope.

Besides, she consoled herself, unless one counted those few kisses and caresses their first evening in Cascais, Vince had made no effort to make love to her. Chances were he would have emerged from the shower and sent her packing to her own room with a reminder of the time and the fullness of their day's schedule.

A glance at her watch, which he had not removed from her wrist last night, told her she should get dressed. The early bus for Sintra left Cascais in one hour and fifteen minutes, which made for a hurried breakfast.

The printed fabric of her sundress was predominantly lilac with tiny flowers in shades of blue strewn over the background. Ruffles of coarse cream-colored eyelet lace made an exaggerated pretense of demureness and added to the charm of the dress, which exposed the light tan she had acquired yesterday on the beach. For a while this morning she would need the knit cardigan in a matching shade of lilac. Fortunately, her low-heeled white sandals were comfortable as well as appropriate to the femininity of her outfit.

"You have a rare trait of punctuality," Vince complimented when she opened the door to his light tap, ready to go. His eyes spoke of a different appreciation, though, as he gazed at her.

On the previous evening they had agreed it would be quicker to eat breakfast in the dining room than to have it brought up to either of their rooms. Walking beside Vince in the corridor and riding in the elevator to the first floor, Alex was able to avoid contact with his eyes. So far there had not been even a passing reference to the previous evening or to her precipitate flight this morning. The subject seemed to hang awkwardly between them, making it impossible for her to feel and act natural with him.

The dining room was set up for breakfast and the service was very prompt. A waiter came and asked for their preference of coffee or tea and returned almost immediately with a steaming pot of coffee and a large pitcher of hot milk. A basket of rolls, butter, and fruit preserves already sat on the table.

Alex busied herself with a roll, feeling the weight of Vince's gaze as he watched every movement of her hands. Irritated with herself for allowing him to disconcert her to the extent that she couldn't perform a simple task like spread preserves on her roll without dropping a blob on the tablecloth, she forced herself to look up. But she could read nothing in his dark eyes.

When he finally spoke, his tone was grave. "I know what's on your mind," he said. "And I can put your worries to rest."

Her heart pounded with a wild suspense when he paused as though waiting for some reply. "Y–you c–can," she stuttered, filled with uncertainty as to what to expect. She wouldn't have been surprised at derision or irony or even the playful teasing so familiar by now, but the gravity of his tone flooded her with inexplicable dread of what she might hear next.

"On the basis of last night, I can assure you unequivocally that you do not snore in your sleep." The lashes swept upward and revealed dark devils of mischief in his eyes. Only then did Alex realize he had been putting her on.

She searched for a suitably devastating retort and finally had to make do with a mock show of relief at his revelation. "You just can't *imagine* how I've worried!"

After that interchange, the tension between them was gone, dissolved by shared laughter. In the privacy of her own reflections, Alex was sure Vince had known the real reasons for her awkwardness and had deliberately taken steps to dispel it, using his incredible intuition to know just what to do or say to put a person at ease.

Underneath her relief that she could now laugh and talk with all the former lack of self-consciousness throbbed a persistent disappointment that once again

Vince had adroitly side-stepped a confrontation that
would bring into the open the source of her puzzlement
and growing frustration. She *knew* he was attracted to
her as she was to him, and yet they had slept in the same
room last night in separate beds.

Why?

She had as few answers as ever, but a new resolve
hardened inside her. Up until now she had not resisted
when he switched the subject to a safer topic or wielded
with consummate skill the tool of his wit to circumvent
a straight answer to a probing question. Somehow she
would think of a method of forcing him to be honest
with her. The details of this resolution very soon were
left entirely to her subconscious as the bus ride came to
demand the participation of all her senses, and she forgot
everything else in the exhilarating immediacy of the present.

The road to Sintra was narrow and serpentine, twisting
and dipping and climbing along the coast so that each
spectacular vista of the ocean was followed by one even
more awesome. The bus ride was also very physical—
something like taking a ride on a giant roller coaster.

The bus driver undoubtedly was a spiritual cousin of
the daredevil taxi drivers she had encountered in Lisbon.
He was utterly undaunted by curves that wound around
the edges of cliffs as the bus climbed steadily upward
into the mountains. In all situations that held the peril
of unseen approaching vehicles, his alternative to slowing
down was to sound loud warning blasts on the horn.

They passed through quaint villages and in one tiny
hamlet they came face to face with another bus. After
a silent staring session between the two unyielding drivers, some unspoken decision was reached. The other bus
backed up until they were able to squeeze past each other
with mere inches to spare.

"This bus ride should be a *must* for all our Globe
travelers who visit Sintra!" Alex insisted laughingly,
bouncing against Vince as the bus hit a rough patch of

pavement in the middle of a curve that brought them back into the open. From there they had an unobstructed view over the side of the mountain and could see villages through which they had passed, tiny clusters of white and orange nestled in the green folds of valleys. In the distance they could see the vast blue expanse of the Atlantic Ocean.

They got off the bus in the center of Sintra, in front of the City Palace. They took a tour of the palace, which had housed royalty up until 1910. Once it had been the summer palace of Moorish sultans, and even though the original structures had been torn down since then, the Moorish style of architecture had been incorporated in the rebuilding, especially visible in the cool shaded interior patios accented by the tinkle of fountains.

The palace was a sumptuous testimony to an era of wealth, to a time when Portuguese explorers had plundered the riches of the world. There were priceless treasures in abundance: rare porcelain and jade from the Orient, huge tapestries and rugs, elaborately carved, and inlaid furniture. The azulejos, or glazed earthenware tiles, on the walls were, the guide droned, the most beautiful in all of Portugal, and the oil paintings were by known masters.

Following the guide from room to room with a small group of tourists, Alex tried to imagine real flesh-and-blood people living in the midst of all the stiffly formal elegance; she failed dismally. Then in the middle of the tour, she had a thought so disquieting that after it she comprehended very little of the guide's routine explanations. Perhaps the thought occurred as a byproduct of a morbid sensitivity aroused by tramping through rooms and viewing surroundings once enjoyed by real people who were now insubstantial shades lingering in the background or peering from time-darkened portraits on the walls. Whatever the reason, the thought slithered into her consciousness with cold reptilian stealth: in an appallingly short time this visit to Portugal would be over. Her work with Vince would be completed, and they would return to the States. What would happen then? Would he go his way and she hers? The prospect of separation brought a sharp pain to her chest and involuntarily she pressed the spot with one hand tensed into a fist.

"What's wrong?" A note of concern in Vince's low voice made her aware that the involuntary movement had not gone unnoticed. The clean familiar scent of him in her nostrils increased her mood of desolation.

"Indigestion," she lied in a hoarse rasping whisper which hurt her tight throat muscles. Then she pretended a close attention to the guide's monologue.

The intensity of her own reaction to the idea of parting from Vince in the near future shocked her deeply. Was it possible that what she felt toward him went far beyond physical attraction, as strong as that undoubtedly was? Could she—without even being aware of what was happening to her—have fallen in love with the same man she had spurned years earlier?

The dizzying spiral of her thoughts increased her agitation, and by the time the tour was completed and the group had emerged into the bright sunlight, her features were pale and strained. Vince's concern would not be brushed aside with her assurance that she was perfectly all right and ready to take a taxi up to the Pena Palace, which they planned to visit before lunch. He took a firm grasp on her arm and ushered her across the street to an open air cafe.

"I'm perfectly all right now," Alex insisted again a few minutes later as she sipped at the Coke he had ordered for her. And indeed she was feeling much better, with the sunshine streaming down with a warmth that caused her to shed the light cardigan and expose her neck and shoulders and arms to the consoling rays. Common sense had returned and urged her to push aside any thought of the future that might spoil her total pleasure in the present. She decided with some firmness to let tomorrow take care of itself.

"Aren't those horses perfectly gorgeous and those fancy little carriages handsome?" she commented, looking across the street where several paired teams were harnessed to open buggies painted in bright colors.

Vince followed her gaze and agreed. "What would you say to the idea of riding up to the Pena Palace in one of those?" he suggested, taking her completely by surprise.

"Why, yes!" she agreed immediately and then felt consciencebound to ask if it wouldn't be far more expensive than a regular taxi. He shrugged aside that reservation and a few minutes later was helping her up into the seat behind the stolid driver's higher perch.

The horses' hooves clip-clopped smartly against the cobbles paving the crooked, narrow streets as they left the City Palace. At first there were tiny shops set into the ground floors of narrow buildings with grillwork balconies overflowing with clay pots of flowering plants. Then there were small villas overrun with bougainvillaea and wisteria. Alex could easily understand now why Lord Byron had referred to Sintra as a "glorious Eden." Luxuriant vegetation grew everywhere in charming, rambling disorder: purple bougainvillaea, crimson geraniums, wisteria, and countless other blossoms she could not name added brilliant color and wonderful fragrance to the lush green of shrubbery and dense tree foliage abounding everywhere.

Once they were out of town and climbing a road which wound steadily upward, there was no sign of people, only verdant forest on either side of them. The air was fresh and sweet, as intoxicating to Alex as a draught of cool vintage wine.

"Isn't this great fun!" she demanded, not wanting to disclose the main ingredient of her enjoyment of their ride. She would willingly have ridden all day through this beautiful countryside with utter contentment as long as Vince was close beside her. She could feel the hard imprint of his thigh against her own. Now and then when the buggy ran over a bump in the road, his arm, placed across the back of their seat, was jostled into warm contact with her shoulder.

"If I were rich, I'd do nothing but travel from one fascinating place to another!" she declared with passionate fervor. It was an impetuous statement, made in an excess of high spirits, and she hadn't really meant it. When he didn't make any comment, she began to worry that she may have sounded resentful of having to work for a living.

"Since I'm not rich, the next best thing is working and traveling for you, Vince," she added in an impulsive effort to correct whatever wrong impression she might have unwittingly created. The muscles of his thigh tightened into cords of steel under the hand she placed, without any intent of provocation, on the long leg next to hers.

"How does a husband fit into your globe-trotting aspirations?"

His question, spoken in a quiet, thoughtful tone, acted violently upon Alex's emotions, at first buoying her to dizzying heights at the possibility that he might have a personal interest in her answer. Then, like a deflated balloon, she dropped back to earth, realizing he undoubtedly had a legitimate reason to inquire into her marital plans. Globe Travel was spending considerable money training her, and as its owner, he would want to know if she planned to remain with the job.

"Not too well," she quipped, and was saved from the need for further reply by their arrival at the palace, which crowned the top of a hill and embodied most people's ideal of a fairy-tale castle, with towers and turrets and battlemented walls aplenty.

Another guide, as nondescript and mousy in his gray suit as the one at the City Palace, assembled a small group of the visitors milling about and snapping pictures of the sensational view and led them from room to room imparting information. Alex only half listened, preferring to open her mind to her own impressions rather than clutter it with a mass of meaningless data she wouldn't be able to retain for long.

About midway through the tour, the group emerged into dazzling sunshine on a high broad terrace, where they were granted a respite from the organized march from room to room. The view from the terrace was nothing short of inspiring, and there was a frenzy of picture-taking with cameras of every conceivable description. Alex took her own small inexpensive camera from her purse and backed a few steps away from Vince, who was perched on the edge of the thick parapet. Realizing her intentions, he posed rather too obligingly, causing her to giggle and accuse him of being camerastruck.

"Here," he commanded, rising and coming toward her with outstretched hand, "I'll take your picture."

This offer proved to hold complications not visible on the surface of it, and he soon had her convulsed with laughter at his imposture as a professional photographer never quite pleased with his subject's pose. He paced from one vantage point to another, returned several times to lift her chin a trifle or place her hand in a different position. Finally he snapped several shots.

Alex was aware that they were being watched by a strikingly handsome couple she had noticed earlier. Now the young man approached them with a smile and asked Vince, "Would you like me to take a picture of you and your wife together?" His accent identified him immediately as an American.

She gasped when Vince did not correct the young man's mistake but handed him the camera and came over to her with a wicked smile. "We'd love that, wouldn't we, sweetheart?"

He settled next to her on the parapet and pulled her close against him so that her head was cradled against his shoulder and his chin nestled in her hair. "Close your mouth and smile," he murmured in a voice that vibrated with amusement at having taken her so completely unawares.

"Yes, darling," she cooed sweetly and relaxed against the muscular wall of his chest.

Next it was Vince's turn to take a picture of the young couple, who readily accepted the offer, volunteering with happy smiles, "We're on our honeymoon too." *Too*! Alex's startled eyes met Vince's, which showed great amusement. She pondered the couple's assumption while she watched Vince adjust their expensive camera and then take several pictures of them together, their honeymoon status blatantly apparent to her in the way they looked at each other and kept their fingers entwined.

What had caused them to conclude that she and Vince were newly married? It was a question of such boundless fascination that she heard nothing of what the guide said during the remainder of the tour.

"What are you thinking about?" Vince whispered in her ear at one point.

"I haven't seen a single comfortable piece of furniture, have you?" she whispered back, and marveled at the remarkable facility with which she produced an answer so far from the truth.

The innocent charade Vince had played with the young honeymooners had introduced a fantasy Alex found thrilling in all its implications as she imagined what it would be like to be Vince's wife. How wonderful it would be to have a husband one could respect as well as love, for if she wasn't already in love with Vince, she was sure she could be if given the faintest hope of reciprocation.

At some point during the day, following the picture-taking episode with the young honeymooners and its titillating pretense, she conceived a plan. And its utter audacity filled her with nervous elation every time she thought about it! Perhaps the main source of inspiration was the assumption made by the young couple that she and Vince were married: their mistake seemed to lend an outside credence to her own strong intuition that he was not physically indifferent to her. No doubt the thought which had plagued her earlier in the day—the briefness of the time remaining for her and Vince to be together in Portugal—added a sense of urgency which helped bolster the courage she would need to carry out her plan.

The last bus departing Sintra for Cascais was scheduled to leave the town square at four o'clock. It was parked in readiness in front of the City Palace at a quarter to four. Some of the passengers had already boarded, but Alex and Vince chose to remain outside until the last minute.

"Excuse me, I'll be back in a minute," Alex murmured, knowing that he thought her immediate mission was a visit to the public rest room across the street in the tourist information office. She deliberately strengthened that impression by walking across the street in that direction.

Glancing back over her shoulder and seeing that he was no longer watching her, she darted around a corner into a side street lined with shops serving the tourist trade. The maze of narrow, crooked streets was ready-made for her purpose, which was to elude Vince if he decided to come after her. When she judged she had walked far enough, she ducked into a shop whose entrance was so cluttered with articles on display that a passerby couldn't see into the interior.

Her heart pounded painfully against her rib cage, and she took a few deep breaths to try to calm the torrent of blood rushing through her veins. Trying not to consider the possibility of her plan backfiring in her face, she picked up some postcards without even really inspecting them and paid the clerk with hands that trembled.

A consultation of her watch showed that she would do well to browse a few minutes more. There was always the risk that Vince, with his persuasive powers, might convince the driver to delay his departure.

When she finally deemed it time to return to the square, she had some difficulty in retracing the route she had taken earlier, and several wrong turns made her considerably later than she had intended to be. Vince was standing in approximately the same place she had left him, looking so thunderous that her heart leaped up into her throat.

He watched her as she crossed the street clutching her parcel in full view. "Oh dear. I'm so sorry! I guess I caused us to miss the bus." Her agitation increased under the narrow-eyed suspicion with which he regarded her, and she tried to cover her nervousness with more words. "I wanted to buy some postcards as mementos from Sintra and I guess I must have lost track of the time." Her voice sounded appallingly thin and unconvincing, even to her own ears.

"You'll have to come up with a more original story than that, Alex." Icy disapproval pelted her skin like a driving winter sleet in February. "You knew that was the last bus to Cascais until tomorrow morning. Why did you deliberately cause us to miss it?" he demanded harshly. She noticed that his hands were tightened into fists and the bones of his knuckles shone death white.

"It was such fun this afternoon at the Pena Palace pretending to be honeymooners . . . and it won't be long before this time in Portugal will be over. . . . I thought— I mean, couldn't we . . . pretend a little longer to be—"

"I don't *want* to play at being married to you, Alex," he interrupted savagely, and the words seemed to have been ground out between his set teeth.

This caustic rejection of her halting proposition had the effect of molten lava pouring over her. *He sounded as if he hated her*! Trembling with the raw anguish of that thought, Alex struggled to hold back the tears which were blinding her vision and causing an ache at the back of her throat. She lost the battle and lowered her head in yet another defeat.

"I'm sorry, Vince," she said in a voice muffled by the degrading tears. "I felt so *happy* here today. I didn't want to go back...it seemed like a good idea..." She yearned to explain to him the complex web of feelings that had led her to do what she had done, but the trickle of tears developed into a full-fledged torrent which she fought to abate.

He didn't speak for a moment, and when he did, he no longer sounded so angry and he seemed not even to be talking to her but to himself. "What's done is done, and it's not as though it's the end of the world. I just have to decide now what to do."

The note of weary indecision was strangely disquieting in one so consummately sure of himself, so capable of making decisions with none of the vacillation Alex had criticized in herself. What was it he had said to her just yesterday? *I always know immediately what I want.*

Oblivious to the wet streaks staining her cheeks, Alex looked up anxiously at him, her long bronze-tipped lashes sticking together in jagged spikes. "Couldn't we rent a car and drive back to Cascais?" she asked tentatively, all thought gone now except the desire to win somehow his forgiveness and undo the wrong she had wrought in her impulsiveness. She hadn't once dreamed he would be this upset by a disruption in their itinerary—the violence of his first reaction was so out of keeping with his whole philosophy of flexible travel plans.

He looked down at her and then quickly transferred his gaze to a spot far away. The dismaying conviction that he could no longer even tolerate the sight of her threatened to produce a fresh onslaught of tears.

"We could hire a taxi to take us back to Cascais this afternoon," he said in that same reflective voice, as if he were talking aloud to himself. "But there's a remote possibility we might be able to find hotel accommodations here without a reservation."

"What would you advise your clients to do under the

same circumstances?" Alex urged timidly, trying to be helpful.

"*My clients*?"

She found the undertone of savage irony in his voice totally inexplicable since her question seemed to her entirely reasonable in view of the circumstances. She endured with a quaking heart his probing scrutiny of her features, wondering fearfully what his thoughts were behind that bronze mask and dreading that he might disclose them to her. Something in her tear-bright eyes or the uncertain tremulousness of her mouth must have aided him in coming to a decision.

"The most practical course of action for my clients would *not* be to stand around and waste valuable time," he said gently, and then to Alex's incredible relief, he actually smiled at her. "Let's see if we can find a place to sleep, and if that doesn't work out, we'll look for an enterprising taxi driver."

She was flooded with relief at this reappearance of the sure, decisive Vince who would be able to handle whatever came up. Simultaneously she was smitten with compunction as his last words made her realize how exorbitantly expensive it would be to hire a taxi to drive them back to Cascais. They would have to pay a driver double fare to cover his return trip. If that became necessary, she vowed firmly to herself, she would insist upon paying the expense herself. It was only right under the circumstances.

In her inexperience she envisioned the two of them tramping from one hotel to another searching for a vacancy, but of course Vince's method was far more efficient. He explained their problem to the hall porter at the first small inn they came to. The man readily offered his services even though his hotel was fully booked, and after several telephone calls, he had located a room. It was available, he explained, only because of a last-minute cancellation.

"I have asked that the room be held for you, but you should go immediately and claim it," he advised, pocketing Vince's generous tip with a pleased expression.

They found the old-fashioned two-story hotel without any difficulty. Alex was secretly charmed with its large, high-ceilinged reception rooms and abundance of dark polished wood, but she was still too chastened by the memory of Vince's recent anger to show her enthusiasm.

He filled out the registration card and left his passport with the hall porter, explaining that they would be back after they had purchased a few articles necessary for the night. Since they had no luggage to deposit in the room and could hardly afford to turn it down if it failed to meet their usual standards, they left the hotel without even inspecting the room.

Thus, it wasn't until they returned to the hotel and went upstairs to freshen up before dinner that Alex saw her first double bed in Europe. It brought home to her the reality of what she had done, of the situation into which she had forced them.

Plagued by a vague tension that she seemed unable to dispel, she was relieved when Vince suggested almost immediately that they go down to the little lounge on the first floor and have a drink before dinner. The host was there and acting as bartender. Soon Alex was drawn into conversation with several of the other guests present.

Dinner was served family style at several large round tables in the dining room adjoining the lounge. The food smelled and looked appetizing, but by now tension had formed a tightly coiled knot inside Alex's stomach and she had great difficulty forcing down even a few bites; after doing so, she fought to control rising waves of nausea.

She was remembering now with distressing clarity the terrible sense of failure that had caused her to regard sex with increasing repugnance and dread during the years of her marriage. The thought of returning with Vince to that room upstairs, and its double bed, filled her with panic.

She was aware of Vince's eyes on her from time to time throughout the meal, and it was no wonder considering the strangeness of her behavior. Offering nothing to the conversation at their table and after those first few bites managing to sustain the merest pretense of eating, she occupied herself with pushing the food around on her plate.

After an eternity, the meal was finally over and chairs were pushed back amid exclamations of contentment and compliments to the cook, who was the owner's wife. Some of the guests made their intention clear to return to the lounge for a liqueur while they watched television or played cards. Several others protested that after a meal like that some exercise was definitely in order.

Seizing upon any excuse not to return to the room upstairs, Alex suggested joining this latter group for a walk. The husky intensity of her voice caused Vince's eyes to narrow speculatively as they met her feverishly bright ones.

"Would you mind very much if we don't?" he replied evenly. "We've already walked a considerable number of miles today, and you hardly ate enough to feel the need of an after-dinner stroll."

She seemed to have little alternative other than to acquiesce, and with a sensation of doom verging on irrational terror, she accompanied him upstairs. As soon as the door closed behind them, she realized how ineffectually she had managed to conceal from Vince the cause of her anxiety.

Angry words erupted from him. "I really don't understand what your game is, Alex. You landed the two of us in this room together—for some reason I can't quite fathom—and now you're acting like a nervous bride who's decided to duck out just after the ceremony." He walked a few steps away from her toward the center of the room and remained with his back to her so that she could not see his expression. "You're going to have to make up your mind now whether you still want to stay here tonight. I need to make one thing perfectly clear. If we stay, I intend to make love to you."

She stared at his back, the words ringing in her ears, the undertone of anger clearly evident. She couldn't blame him in the least for being provoked at her behavior—she *was* acting like an hysterical bride on her wedding night. The main difference was that her fear was based on humiliating experience not ignorance, and she didn't know if she had the courage to make herself vulnerable in that way again.

For a moment she wavered, unsure of what to do. What if she chose to return to Cascais? The answer seemed chillingly clear to her—she would have lost forever this opportunity to achieve the closeness she longed to share with Vince. As he had so bluntly reminded her, she had deliberately "landed them in this room together" and she wanted desperately to stay and have what happened between them prove to be beautiful and right.

She would stay.

"Do you mind if I use the bathroom first?" She fled before seeing the searching force of his look as he wheeled around to face her.

When she came back into the room a few minutes later, it was plunged into what seemed to her strained senses a Stygian darkness, but gradually she was able to make out the long length of him in the bed. And then her eyes adjusted to the dimness, and she could see by the faint illumination of moonlight filtering through the open window that he lay on his back with his hands clasped behind his head.

He said nothing, and a shy embarrassment swept her at the realization that he could see well enough in the silvery dimness to know she had removed all her clothes in the bathroom and stood naked before him.

Unable to think of anything to say that might relieve the unbearable tension in the room, she climbed into the bed on the opposite side from him and pulled the sheet up to her neck. Her strongest emotion at that moment was a deep self-loathing. Here she was in bed with the man whose compelling masculine attractiveness had kept her awake more often than not since she had arrived in Portugal, and she was powerless by word or touch to breach the yawning gulf separating them, though their bodies were mere inches apart.

She was dimly aware that he had turned on his side toward her, and then she felt the weight of his arm placed across her body on top of the sheet. "My God, you're actually trembling," he muttered roughly and gathered her close to him as he would a frightened child. He stroked her with soothing gentleness while he cursed himself with a low violence that caused her great distress.

"Please don't blame yourself," she pleaded, placing her fingers over his lips. "It's not your fault. It's just *me*."

He was quiet then and she snuggled closer to him, thrilling to the warmth and security of being held in his arms. She had no reliable concept of time, but it seemed to her the dissipation of her nervousness was fairly rapid as she became increasingly aware of the intimacy of her bare flesh against his hard muscular length.

Indulging a long-suppressed desire to be free with his body, she reached up and ran her palm experimentally along the breadth of his powerful shoulders and then trailed it down the smoothly muscled contours of his back. His flesh was firm and resilient to her stroking touch, and she pulled back from him slightly so that she could explore the hard wall of his chest before sliding her palm appreciatively over his taut stomach.

The sensual pleasure she was deriving from the touch of his firm flesh under her hands speedily banished her timidity, and her caresses grew deliberately provocative,

invested with the intent to arouse. She felt the tell-tale
tremor of his muscles under her fingers, but he made no
effort to touch her in return.

Baffled and beginning to suffer the initial stages of
physical frustration at his inexplicable passiveness—after
all, he had said he would make love to her if she stayed—
she raised one hand and stroked the hard plane of his
cheek and pressed her lips against his encouragingly. His
mouth was firm and cool and unresponsive, even when
she made an experimental little foray with the tip of her
tongue.

"Please—make love to me, Vince," she pleaded with
a note of desperation.

His arms tightened convulsively, drawing her so hard
against his entire length that she had undeniable proof
of her success in arousing him. She had begun to wonder
about the state of her ribs when his hold loosened and
his hands and lips began a slow, maddeningly sensual
exploration of her body that left her weak and totally
captive to his touch. He kissed and caressed every part
of her, igniting her flesh with a languorous fire that made
her moan aloud and whisper his name in helpless passion.

His tongue teased the nipples of her breasts until they
were hard and tingling and ached for the total possession
of his mouth, which surely was guided by an erotic obsession to inflame every inch of her body. Her remaining
inhibitions vanished in a rising spiral of exquisite tension,
and she sought to imitate his actions, wanting to impart
to him the same intense sensations he had awakened to
throbbing life in her. But what she started for his pleasure
became her own joyful, mindless discovery, and she
recognized a voice as her own as it cried out, "Please,
Vince—now!"

Afterward her rational mind would have to reject the
overwhelming sense of surprise: *this has never happened
to me before*! The impression of a totally new discovery
was dominant, as though she were making love for the

first time. Her need and his were the same, their breath came in deep, gasping unison, their bodies merged into a single entity of pulsating, all-encompassing sensation.

The fast spiraling acceleration of her whole being toward a shattering cataclysm of release was devastatingly new and miraculous, as was the unbelievably sweet sense of wholeness and tender warmth afterward when she lay in Vince's arms. A rapturous voice sang from somewhere deep inside her: *I love this man! Oh, how I love this man!* She went to sleep to the lilting music.

When she awoke the next morning, her lips were curved into a smile and her body was heavy with a languorous sensation of well-being. It took only a second to identify the source of hard, masculine warmth as Vince's body pressed against her own and to recall the impassioned love-making which had all the magic of a miracle for her. She had never dreamed it could be like that!

The love she had discovered in the height of her passion last night throbbed in her breast with every breath she drew as she lay beside Vince and watched him. He looked so incredibly unguarded in sleep, his mouth and jawline relaxed and vulnerable as she had never seen them in waking. It required all of her self-control not to reach over and stroke her fingers along the hard angles and planes covered now with a dark stubble, not to press her lips against his, slightly parted in sleep.

Suddenly he opened his eyes and fixed them upon her. She watched the opaque blankness transform swiftly into recognition and then held her breath as some powerful, indefinable emotion flared up in the dark depths of his eyes. He lowered his lashes and she wondered dazedly if she had only imagined it.

Remembering his anger yesterday when she caused them to miss the bus, she wished he would say something to reassure her that he was now glad for what had happened between them. But he seemed deeply absorbed in his waking thoughts, whatever they were, and didn't speak at all as he turned away from her onto his back and gazed up at the ceiling.

Alex could suddenly no longer contain her need for reassurance. "You're not *sorry* that this happened, are you, Vince?" she asked anxiously, raising herself up on one elbow so that she could see his face and perhaps read his expression.

He turned his head and his dark eyes lingered on her face a moment before dropping lower to the delectable curves of her bare breasts. Until then she hadn't even been aware that the sheet had dropped to her waist, and she didn't try to cover herself.

"I awake to find an enchantress in my bed, and you ask if I'm sorry," he said huskily, a smile lurking around his lips. Later she would try to recall the exact intonations of his voice and realize he hadn't really answered her question at all, but now her anxieties were banished as he pulled her down on top of his chest, and her lips met his in a kiss that quickly deepened and resurrected her passion.

With the early morning sunshine streaming into the room and highlighting strands of gold in Alex's tawny hair, they made love again.

Chapter Seven

ALEX CHIDED HERSELF for being so superstitious as she took the black dress from its hanger and slipped it over her head. It was the only gown she had packed that was sufficiently sophisticated and glamorous for dining and dancing at the Estoril Casino and then later visiting the gambling rooms. How absurd of her to remember the night in Lisbon when she had last worn the dress.

Her purpose had been to pierce Vince's masculine armor and make him aware of her as a woman. The evening at the O'Faia Club had led her to think she had been successful, and she had ridden back to the hotel high on wine and the heady elixir of feminine conquest only to be dashed cruelly to the ground when Vince bade her a distant, polite goodnight outside the elevator. Just remembering that evening, she felt the sharp pangs of rejection all over again.

Closing the long back zipper, Alex sighed, admitting to herself the real truth behind the pervasive gloominess of her mood as she dressed for what should be a gala night. *This was her last evening in Portugal with Vince.* That constant, throbbing thought was like an abscess festering in her mind, making her pensive and filling her with apprehensions.

Ever since her first evening in Portugal—could that possibly have been only thirteen days ago?—she seemed to have been stalking something continually elusive to her grasp. At first she had identified her needs as purely physical and had pondered ways, finally even connived in Sintra, to get Vince into bed with her. And as undeniably glorious as making love with him had turned out to be, she still wasn't satisfied—she still hadn't penetrated those psychic barriers with which he swathed himself.

In spite of the increased physical intimacy between them, she knew the private person inside Vince no better than she had before he made love to her. And not once had he mentioned love, his restraint causing her to bottle up her own powerful feelings for him until she sometimes felt as if she would explode if she kept them to herself any longer.

Inspecting her make-up and giving a last-minute pat to the lustrous wings of tawny hair which almost brushed the smooth tan of her shoulders, Alex sighed again and met the gaze of the unhappy hazel eyes looking out at her from the mirror. It wasn't that she wanted a marriage proposal from Vince. She hadn't gone into their relationship with any expectation of permanency. But she *did* want desperately for him to tell her he cared for her, that she meant something more to him than just a partner in a casual affair. If she could be assured that their relationship had some dimension for him beyond the purely physical, as it certainly did for her, she would be happy to continue as they were, without legal ties, once they returned to the States.

As matters were now, there had been no mention of any future beyond their day-to-day itinerary—what they would do the following day, where they would go, how they would get there. And very soon there wouldn't even be the occasion for that: tomorrow they would be returning to Lisbon and from there to New York City. After they reached Kennedy Airport, Alex didn't even know where Vince would be going next.

These somber thoughts were interrupted by the shrill ring of the telephone. She answered with an eager "Hello," expecting to hear Vince's voice. Instead she heard the polite tones of the hall porter relaying a request for her to please meet Mr. Reardon in the bar when she was ready.

This unexpected departure from their usual routine might have served as an omen to Alex that nothing about her last evening in Portugal would turn out the way she hoped. She had been dressed for several minutes and only waiting for Vince to tap on her door as he invariably did. *Why* had he gone down to the bar for a drink without even checking first to see if she might not also be ready?

Standing on the threshold of the small combination bar and lounge a few minutes later, she saw him sitting up at the L-shaped bar deep in conversation with the bartender and another customer. The bartender whisked away an empty glass from in front of Vince and replaced it with a full one on a fresh napkin. Obviously he hadn't just arrived.

The bartender's polite smile and nod of greeting in Alex's direction called Vince's attention to her presence, and he slid courteously to his feet, looking very tall and formal in a dark suit. Since their arrival in Cascais, she had become accustomed to seeing him in jeans and cotton-knit shirts and his transformation back to business executive was a sharp reminder to Alex of her status as his employee.

She shook her head when he inquired politely if she would prefer to sit at one of the sofas away from the bar and came over to perch on the stool next to him. The man on his other side was noticeably restless at this interruption in their conversation and resumed it as soon as possible. Alex ordered a glass of white wine and listened.

The drink in front of Vince was emptied in a very short time and he ordered another one. Before tonight, Alex had rarely seen him drink anything except wine and beer and this suddenly revealed liking for Scotch surprised her.

Instead of inducing high spirits, though, the drinks seemed to make him increasingly taciturn and withdrawn. By the time he helped Alex into the taxi summoned to drive them to the casino in nearby Estoril, his manner was extremely remote, as though his thoughts were miles removed. His speech and physical coordination showed no signs of inebriation, however.

At first, Alex waged a desperate battle against the spiritual oppression weighing her down. It was as though she hoped that by acting natural herself, continuing to talk and laugh with her customary enthusiasm, she could strike some responsive chord in Vince. But the effort took its toll on her nerves, and by the time they arrived at the casino, she was so tightly strung and tense that her voice sounded shrill to her own ears.

Now will the real *Vince Reardon please stand up!* she thought with a touch of bitter hysteria later as they sat at a table in the huge, palatial restaurant. On the surface, everything about this last dinner in Europe was glamorous and perfect. The setting was elegant, the food superbly prepared and flawlessly served, their fellow diners composed of exquisitely dressed women and suave, attentive men. Yet to Alex there was a brittle, hollow ambience about it, as if they were all actors in a strange, stylized drama, playing out their individual roles of civility.

Her sense of unreality persisted even when she danced in Vince's arm to the music of the orchestra. He danced well, showing the same effortless assurance with which he did everything, and yet there was such impersonality in his touch that he might well have been an accomplished paid escort and she a wealthy socialite willing to pay for the semblance of masculine devotion.

By the time dinner was over, she had abandoned all her former efforts at normal conversation. It was a relief when the first show of the evening began. Most of the dancers were women and the numbers they performed were from famous Broadway plays. The costumes were brilliantly colored and glittered with sequins while managing to cover the barest minimum of gyrating, bouncing female flesh.

Alex privately considered most of what she saw up on the stage just a slicker, more expensive version of what she imagined a strip-tease show was like.

"What did you think of it?" she asked Vince when the show was over. He had remained so utterly impassive during the entire hour she had been unable to read his reaction or even to ascertain if he were really watching the seductive movements in front of his eyes.

"It reminded me of shows I've seen in Las Vegas," he replied indifferently and signaled to a waiter who was hovering watchfully nearby.

Alex had to stifle her surprise when he ordered coffee for her and a Scotch and water for himself. Once again he was diverging from the usual pattern, for normally he also liked coffee after dinner, sometimes with a glass of cognac. Why, she wondered, was he drinking so heavily this evening, especially since it only seemed to deepen his somberness?

Just before midnight they left the restaurant and went to the gambling rooms in another part of the building. At the massive double entrance doors they had to show their passports and buy observers' tickets, since they did not plan to gamble. Alex had firmly denied any interest when Vince inquired if she would like to try her luck at the tables. She just wanted to watch firsthand what before she had seen only in movies or television programs.

Aside from the superb French crystal chandeliers suspended from the ceiling, the rooms were much plainer than she had expected, with dark red carpet underfoot and sedate wood paneling on the walls. The dealers and operators, however, looked exactly the way she expected them to look, smooth and professional in their tuxedos. Beneath their blank, bored expressions she sensed an underlying alertness to every move being made at their tables.

As for the patrons, they might have been playing checkers or gin rummy at a small town recreation hall for all the emotion they showed. It was difficult for Alex to comprehend the value of the brightly colored plastic chips and rectangular bars stacked neatly in front of the players.

She stopped at a roulette table more crowded than the others. Even to her inexperienced eyes, the betting seemed to be heavy. Careful not to get in the way, she stood a little behind a heavy-set blond man and watched the blur of the spinning wheel slow until the ivory ball quieted its staccato clatter and settled into a pie-shaped slot.

The blond man evidently had been a big winner, judging from the pile of chips one of the operators shoved across the table toward him. Intrigued with the lack of visible emotion, Alex edged a bit closer. These people greeted the loss of hundreds—maybe thousands, for all she knew—of dollars with at most a raised eyebrow or a faint grimace, while the winners seemed prosaically resigned to their good fortune.

Just then the blond man glanced sideways and grinned at her as if he had known she was there all the time. She could see now the charged excitement in his eyes and knew he wasn't as blasé about winning as she had at first thought.

"Don't go away, Lady Luck," he murmured. "You should wear diamonds on that lovely neck."

Startled and bemused, she looked over her shoulder to see if Vince had observed this little scene straight out of a Hollywood script, but he wasn't behind her. Instinctively she looked around the room and saw him approaching the blackjack tables over on the right side of the large room. A beautiful brunette woman playing at one of the tables looked up and recognized him.

"Vince, darling!" she called out huskily, and to Alex's ears the sound reverberated through the room. She raised deeply tanned bare arms in a gesture that was both invitation and command, and then Alex could see little but the broad expanse of Vince's back and the woman's jeweled hands clasped around his neck as he bent over and kissed her. Judging from the length of time, it was no mere peck on the cheek, and Alex felt her heart sinking like a leaden weight as she watched. Then Vince straightened, reaching up to remove the hands clinging to his neck as he did so.

Alex tore her mesmerized gaze away from him for fear he would turn around and catch her staring with her heart in her eyes. The man next to her had evidently won another huge pile of chips, and she hadn't even been aware of the spin of the wheel. Forcing a smile in response to his, she was too numb to protest when he encircled her waist loosely with his arm and pulled her into the inner ring of players either sitting or standing along the edge of the table. At the moment she was grateful for any excuse not to have to seek out Vince, who apparently had forgotten she existed.

The winning streak her companion repeatedly attributed to her presence continued during the next half hour, but finally she insisted she must go and find her date. To her surprise, the man, who introduced himself as Lawrence Blair, withdrew from the game immediately and without any discernible reluctance. He said he wanted to buy her and her boyfriend a drink as soon as he got a receipt for his stacks of plastic bars at the cashier's window.

"Please," he cajoled with convincing charm, "I'm a richer man right this minute, thanks to you."

Under the present circumstances, Alex wasn't inclined to discourage him as she would have done if she hadn't witnessed that greeting between Vince and the beautiful brunette woman and subsequently been deserted by him. Lawrence Blair was a very pleasant man and not unattractive, and some deep instinct told Alex she might be grateful for his presence before the evening was over.

In an incredibly short time that intuition proved to be unerring. They found Vince and his lovely female companion seated close together on a low velvet divan, seemingly oblivious to the rest of the world. Alex was thankful for the firm support of Lawrence's hand on her back when Vince introduced the woman clinging possessively to his arm as Gloria Allen, the same woman who had telephoned him so persistently their first evening in Cascais.

"I'm delighted to meet you, Alex," Gloria purred in her seductively husky voice, extending a beautifully manicured and ring-laden hand toward Alex. "Vince has been telling me what a *valuable* agent you're going to be for his company. And who's your handsome friend here? We tried to get your attention earlier, but you two were thoroughly engrossed in each other."

Alex introduced Lawrence Blair, jealousy and despair convoluting into a tangled knot inside her at the clear insinuation in Gloria's voice and her blatantly proprietorial manner as she stood beside Vince, her arm linked through his. The woman was making it very plain that Alex was nothing more to Vince than an employee while she, Gloria, had obviously more intimate and prior claims.

Lawrence showed no awareness of the subtle undercurrents among his new acquaintances, offering to buy everyone drinks in one of several bars and nightclubs in the casino building. Gloria instantly accepted for all of them, and Vince said nothing, his dark eyes unfriendly

as they flicked over the stockily built blond man re-
counting the story of how his three-day losing streak had
miraculously changed the second Alex began watching
him play.

Alex wished desperately that Vince would take charge
with that easy manner of command she had witnessed
so frequently and inform Gloria and Lawrence that he
and Alex had to return to their hotel in Cascais since
they were scheduled to leave early in the morning for
Lisbon. In the back of her mind there was still the faintest
hope that something could be salvaged of this last evening, which was going so wrong.

But Vince said nothing of the sort and made no effort
to disengage himself from Gloria's arm, leaving Alex
paired off with Lawrence as the four of them left the
gambling rooms. Her new acquaintance was clearly delighted with his assigned role as her escort and exerted
the full force of his charm to entertain her.

What began as the four of them having a drink together
developed into an all-night affair with Vince devoting
himself exclusively to Gloria and leaving Alex to Lawrence's very willing care. The night club Lawrence had
chosen had a lively combo, and he seemed tireless, leading Alex to the small dance floor time after time.

She devoted all her efforts to the appearance of having
a good time, determined not to give the gloating woman
next to Vince the satisfaction of seeing how she ached
with the hurt inflicted by his indifference. She danced
and laughed and openly flirted with Lawrence who, upon
learning of her plans to return to the States the next day,
began trying to convince her to stay longer in Portugal.

"Have a heart, Reardon," Lawrence addressed Vince
when they returned to the table after one such conversation. "I've just discovered the most exciting woman
I've ever met and she tells me she is completely at your
mercy. Couldn't you spare her another week, at the
least?"

"Yes, darling, have a heart," Gloria purred, nuzzling

her cheek against Vince's sleeve so that Alex had to repress a primitive impulse to tear her away from him. "Can't you see your new little worker has found somebody really special?"

"Alex is free to do whatever she wishes," Vince said curtly and lifted his glass to down the remainder of his Scotch.

Alex was too ravaged by the utter indifference in that comment to have the heart to maintain the charade of gaiety. All she wanted now was to escape this intolerable situation where she had to sit and watch Vince with another woman. This whole evening was a total disaster as far as she was concerned, and the insidious threat of tears under her eyelids warned her she should leave immediately and seek the haven of her own room back in Cascais.

"I'm a working woman, Lawrence," she said firmly, "and my regular boss is expecting me back in the office bright and early Tuesday morning. Hopefully, he finds my services a little more indispensable than Mr. Reardon does." She regretted the sharp bitterness which escaped in that last comment and felt the dark scrutiny of Vince's eyes on her face.

"So if you don't mind, Lawrence, would you get me a taxi?" She smiled appealingly at the big blond man. "I really should get an hour or two of sleep, which is about all there is time for now." The hands on her small gold watch told her it wouldn't be long before the sun would be coming up.

"I can do better than that," Lawrence insisted, standing up. "I'll ride with you to your hotel—"

"That won't be necessary, Blair," Vince interrupted brusquely, coming to his feet with a swift movement and towering over the other man, who looked at first startled and then resentful. "Alex came with me, and I'll see she gets back safely."

"Vince, darling," Gloria protested with a pouting expression, "what about me?"

"I'm sure Blair will be willing to see you to your hotel, Gloria." Vince's lips twisted into a sardonic smile.

Neither Gloria nor Lawrence looked especially happy at this arrangement, but there was little either could do. Vince had come out of his lethargy and taken over the situation in the masterful way Alex had hoped for hours earlier. In a matter of seconds, she had said her goodbyes and was striding through the network of corridors beside him with the parting words of the other two still ringing in her ears.

Lawrence had insisted he would look her up in Georgia at the first opportunity, a promise Alex didn't really expect or want him to keep. But it was Gloria's comment that really stung: "Don't forget our date in L. A. next week, Vince darling!" Evidently Vince had not been as secretive with Gloria about his plans as he had been with her. He must be planning to fly to the West Coast, and had arranged to meet Gloria in Los Angeles.

The uniformed doorman at the casino entrance summoned a taxi from those parked across the street. Vince sank down into the back seat next to Alex with a sound that was half deep sigh and half groan and sat slumped, with his head resting on the back of the seat. His posture was the first indication she had seen all evening that he was feeling the effects of the vast quantity of Scotch he had downed.

Bitterness swelled inside Alex as she realized he hadn't been prompted by any feelings for her or jealousy of Lawrence when he insisted on accompanying her back to the hotel himself. He evidently had reached the limits of his physical endurance and needed to return to his own room to collapse. Smarting with hurt, she huddled into the corner farthest away from him and closed her eyes. She had drunk very little throughout the evening and was wide awake, but her head and body throbbed with tiredness and the aftermath of tension.

Not a single word was spoken between them in the taxi or on the way up to their rooms. Alex was so sunken into her own mood of despair that she was surprised when Vince broke the silence outside her room. He had managed to insert her key into the lock after some uncharacteristic clumsiness and stood there for a few seconds looking down at her.

"Did you enjoy your last evening in Portugal, Alex?" he queried softly, his enunciation a little slurred.

The unexpectedness of the question stirred her to the quick and then awoke a surge of puzzled anger. Why had he acted as he had tonight, knowing as he must have that he was spoiling their last night together in Europe? The probable answer brought a stiff smile of pride to her lips and gave her the strength to muster an answer. No doubt he had been afraid she would try to force him into some kind of commitment on this final night together and thus had acted so cold and distant in order to prevent that. Well, he needn't worry any longer—she would put his mind to rest and salve her own wounds.

"I had a marvelous time, Vince. Being free definitely has its advantages, but I don't have to tell *you* that, do I? You've never known what it is to be tied down to one person."

"You're wrong about that, Alex." Again his words were not as distinct as usual, and she could not read his expression as he stared down at her.

"You mean..." Her heart leaped painfully in her chest. What she had dreaded was true—he *was* emotionally committed to someone else.

"I mean it's possible not to be married to a person and still be 'tied down,' as you put it." He sighed and pressed one hand to his forehead. "I'm going to hate myself tomorrow." With that he pushed open her door, leaving her no choice but to enter the room and leave him standing there. The door closed behind her with a little click of finality as the lock engaged.

Perhaps if she had been able to cry it would have helped her to get some relief from the misery engulfing her soul. But her grief and hurt seemed too deep for the release of purging tears. Why hadn't Vince told her before tonight that he was committed to someone else? Why had he found it necessary to subject her to an entire evening of cold indifference to convince her she had no claim on his affections? Considering what she knew of his character, the kindness and considerateness he had shown time after time to her as well as others, she just couldn't understand his actions, and that only intensified her hurt.

She must have dropped off to sleep only a short time before she would have to get up and pack because the knock on her door startled her into groggy awakeness.

"Alex? Are you up?"

She dragged herself over to the door, opened it, and looked out at Vince, who was standing there dressed only in a dark robe. He looked haggard and pale, and her heart ached with sympathy and regret that she couldn't respond the way she would have liked. If things had been different between them, more natural and relaxed, she would have teased him good-naturedly about drinking too much last night and kissed that deep furrow between his eyebrows. As it was, she could only assure him stiltedly that she was awake and would be ready to have her luggage brought down in three-quarters of an hour.

Breakfast was hurried, with a minimum of conversation. Neither of them said much on the train ride to Lisbon either, Vince showing every evidence of having a full-fledged hangover, wincing at each abrupt motion and harsh noise.

Alex was preoccupied with her own thoughts, which were concerned primarily with the question of what she should do when she returned to Stokely. The wonderful job with Globe Travel had backfired in her face when she allowed herself to fall in love with the boss, as she had thought of him before she knew he was someone she had known well in her past. But nothing had changed the necessity of her having to build a career for herself.

Her marriage settlement wouldn't last forever if she lived on it, and she had to support herself. If she quit this job, she would only have to find another one eventually.

On the other hand, if she remained with Globe Travel there would always be the possibility that Vince could walk into the agency on any day, possibly with the woman he loved on his arm, and that eventuality presented serious problems to Alex in her present vulnerable state. Would it not be better for her to sever all connections with Globe Travel, perhaps even move to another town altogether and start over in new surroundings?

It occurred to her in the airport that she and Vince must make a strange pair, both pale with fatigue and hardly speaking to each other, as if they were strangers fate had conspired to make traveling mates. On the airplane he opened his briefcase on his knees and took out several manila files containing papers, which he studied until lunch was served.

Alex finally mustered enough nerve during the meal to ask him about his plans when he arrived in New York, only to have her fears confirmed. He was flying directly to Los Angeles, as Gloria Allen had obviously known last night. Could she possibly be the one to whom Vince was emotionally tied? The thought was unendurable that he could love someone so—so *unworthy* of him.

After lunch, Vince moved his seat into the reclining position and went immediately to sleep. Alex lay back next to him and looked at his sleeping face with a feeling of great tenderness. She would have liked to caress each hard, carved plane of that face, smooth away every ache and pain and worry.

Gradually her own eyelids grew very heavy and she too slept. Sometime later a clinking sound awakened her and she became aware that her cheek rested on a hard, warm surface—Vince's shoulder! During her nap she must have slumped over against him.

She blinked and darted a look upward to see if he was still asleep and met his dark eyes looking down at her with a quizzical expression. It was so typical of the man she had come to love that her heart flooded with new hope. Her lips twitched into a wistful smile and it was everything she could do to keep from murmuring, "Welcome back, Vince darling."

"You're awake in time for a drink before dinner." The crisp matter-of-factness in his tone restored her quickly to her common sense and she sat up, hands going to check the touseled condition of her hair.

"I'll just have a glass of white wine, please." She hoped the huskiness of her voice would be attributed to sleepiness and not the emotions choking her. Waking to find herself pressed against him like that, she had been helpless to prevent the surge of love that licked along her veins and undoubtedly shone from her eyes like a beacon. Coming back to reality—and the futility of her love— was cruel, and she escaped to the privacy of the washroom, pleading the necessity of freshening up before dinner.

When she returned, her glass of wine was waiting for her and Vince was sipping a beer, studying papers in the folders he had perused earlier. If she had dared hope for a return to their former casual intimacy, she was soon aware of the futility of that yearning. At least this new, more formal Vince didn't ignore her altogether as he had last night, downing drink after drink. He discussed several new ideas he had for broadening the scope of Globe Travel, his manner that of a business executive with important matters on his mind. He was the epitome of what she had expected to encounter that first night in Lisbon when she stepped into the lobby at the Hotel Jorge to meet her employer.

Why didn't he maintain that distance from the beginning? A voice of despair railed inside her even as she kept up her end of the conversation with cool poise. *He tried to—he was friendly and aloof*, came the relentlessly honest answer. It had been she, Alex, who had forced their relationship into very intimate channels, and therefore could she blame anyone but herself for the desolation that overwhelmed her as the jet bore her rapidly to a destination that meant separation from Vince?

Tentatively she mentioned to him the next stage of her training, but he dismissed the subject in an offhand manner that cut deeply. "That's Brian's province. He knows his job well. Don't worry."

Alex concentrated on cutting a bite of steak, which looked juicy and was cooked exactly as she had requested—medium rare. It tasted like cardboard, as did the baked potato with sour cream and chives and the broccoli. Vince was making it painfully clear to her that her future meant nothing to him. She was just a new employee who could without doubt be replaced in a matter of hours if her work didn't prove satisfactory.

Pride came to her defense, and she determined that in no way would she reveal to Vince just how much his indifference hurt her. She ate most of the meal without tasting a single bite, watched the full-length movie, and then thumbed through magazines while listening to music through the headphones for the remainder of the flight.

Vince seemed content, perhaps even relieved, to be left to his own thoughts, and he kept busy the entire time readying materials from his briefcase and jotting notes. Several times Alex felt his dark glance, but she pretended to be totally absorbed and didn't even look at him or smile. It had to be a consummate performance worthy of a fine actress, she reflected with bitterness, and one whose success gave her no pleasure whatever.

When the airplane landed in New York City, she learned as they were disembarking that Vince had barely enough time to make the connection with his next flight. He hadn't mentioned that fact earlier, and it filled her with regret when she realized she had only minutes left in his company. Suddenly she was besieged by a powerful urge to tell him how much the past fourteen days had meant to her personally, how it had opened her up to all there was in the world to see and experience outside of her own insulated little niche in Stokely.

But somehow the words were blocked in her throat, and there was actually no opportunity for conversation as they rushed through the throngs of travelers to the front entrance of the big building housing the Portuguese airline on which they had flown. They were fortunate enough to hail a taxi immediately.

The loud beating of her heart seemed to Alex like the slow ticking of a clock measuring off the short span of time left as the taxi drove along the busy street which circled in front of the individual buildings housing the many airlines in the mammoth Kennedy Airport complex. In her imagination, it was as though Vince had already left her, so remote and distant did he seem.

And then the taxi pulled over to the curb and it was time for Vince to get out. Alex felt as if her heart was literally being ripped apart into jagged pieces as he opened the door and put one foot on the pavement. He was going to leave her without a single word to treasure and remember! Suddenly he stopped and looked around at her as if he had just remembered she was there and knew he should speak some polite words of farewell.

His dark eyes touched on her features with lingering intentness, as if he were memorizing them for a mental picture album. "If you become sated on freedom, Alex— change your mind about marrying again—the offer I made you seven years ago is still open." The words were spoken in a low, weary tone that seemed to come from deep inside his chest. He reached out one hand and traced the soft curve of her jaw, and then before she could recover from the shock enough to speak a single word, he was gone, striding through the crowd with loose-limbed grace.

Alex made a small broken sound, like the whimper of an injured animal. The taxi driver glanced curiously at her reflection in his rear-view mirror, but she was totally oblivious to him and to the buildings they were already passing, barely visible through the haze of her tears. Her hand was raised to her face, as if she hoped to capture and retain forever the gentleness of that final fleeting touch.

Chapter Eight

ALEX RAISED THE steaming cup of coffee to her lips and then hastily lowered it as a wave of nausea welled up in her. She got up from the little table in the breakfast alcove of her new apartment and carried the cup over to the sink, where she poured its contents down the drain.

What was wrong with her the last few days that she couldn't bear even the smell of coffee in the morning, when ordinarily she couldn't wait for her first cup to brew? She must have some kind of intestinal virus, or else the nervous strain of the last four weeks was taking a toll on her normally robust health. The latter must be the explanation, because she had never before been irregular in having her period, which had not appeared since her return from Portugal.

She had to get herself together somehow and stop thinking about Vince and that strange last-minute proposal he had made on taking leave of her in New York. She had relived the scene literally thousands of times, trying to fathom his motives and feelings and to understand why he had acted toward her as he had during their last twenty-four hours together. So far she had arrived at no satisfactory conclusions.

It didn't help matters that not once during four weeks had she heard a word from him, either directly by telephone or mail or indirectly through Brian Campbell. She knew the manager of the Stokely office communicated with Vince on a regular basis. It would have been so easy for Vince to at least convey a friendly message, even something as casual as "Tell Alex I said hello." But there was nothing but silence, and Alex kept remembering Gloria Allen's reminder to Vince not to forget their date in Los Angeles. Maybe he had already forgotten Alex's existence in the pleasure of being reunited with Gloria or whoever that woman was who, by his own admission, bound him to her.

But why had he made that strange proposal in New York? She always came back to ponder that seemingly unanswerable question.

Her nausea had subsided by mid-morning and by lunchtime she was ravenous, not having eaten even her usual light breakfast. The hunger pangs were welcomed as an indication that she wasn't after all coming down with a virus. She dismissed all thought of impending illness in her absorption with her work, which she found interesting even from behind a desk. It had come as a revelation to her that people in an ordinary medium-size town like Stokely were as involved in travel, both business and personal, as they were.

But the next morning even the thought of coffee was so repugnant that she tried to get down a cup of hot tea only to have it promptly come back up again. Examining her pale, strained features in the mirror above the sink in the bathroom, Alex shook her head incredulously. What she was thinking just *couldn't* be true, could it?

She couldn't *possibly* be pregnant!

But everything certainly seemed to add up to that. Her missed period, this recurring illness in the morning, her increased appetite later in the day. And it hadn't even occurred to her to take precautions in Portugal, so resigned was she to her inability to conceive.

Wandering slowly back into her bedroom, Alex felt like a battleground of conflicting emotions. The realization that she very likely had within her body Vince's and her child brought a surge of joy that made her momentarily forgetful of the nausea and trembling weakness of her limbs. But then the thought of telling Vince and having him marry her purely out of a sense of duty, loving another woman all the while, brought waves of despair which made her pull the folds of her robe closer around her and huddle miserably on the edge of her unmade bed.

What was she going to do? If she told Vince her situation, there was no doubt whatsoever in her mind that he would insist upon marrying her and taking responsibility for her and the child. But how could she ask him to do something that would ruin his chance of happiness with the person he loved? Hadn't she already done enough to hurt him seven years ago?

What was her alternative to telling him, though? She couldn't possibly stay here in Stokely and have an illegitimate child. She wouldn't subject her parents to that kind of embarrassment, and there was the child to consider too. Around and around her thoughts went, always returning to the same question: what was she going to do?

When she arrived late at the office, pale and haggard under an extra-heavy application of make-up, she was grateful to see her coworkers huddled around one desk looking interestedly at something and talking in excited voices. At least she wouldn't have to undergo their scrutiny and explain her peaked appearance.

"He's a real doll—nice and sooo good-looking!" Jennie Barton cooed in her theatrical manner. It was her desk everyone was gathered around, and she was seated behind it. "Oh, Alex, there you are. Lucky girl—fourteen days in Portugal with this walking dreamboat. Did he mention anything to *you* about a secret engagement?"

Jennie's voice held a faint tinge of some emotion Alex had detected in all the agents in the office since her return but had never been able really to pin down and identify. Was it resentment? Puzzlement? Envy? Or was it some combination of all of these? Right now it was the least of her worries, and she walked over to the desk with a heavy sensation of dread.

Her colleagues opened up a place for her to squeeze in, and she saw what they were peering down at with such avid interest. A magazine lay open and there was a glossy photograph of Vince and Gloria Allen at a party. They were gazing into each other's eyes, as though totally oblivious to the people all around them. The caption read: "Jet-set socialite and travel magnate admit nuptial plans."

Alex felt a tearing sensation in her chest and then her knees buckled under her just as a black fuzziness enveloped her. She felt someone grab her and heard panic in a familiar voice.

"Hey, give me a hand! She's fainted!"

When she came back to consciousness, she was lying supine on the carpet with a ring of anxious faces peering down at her. She smiled weakly. "Sorry to konk out on you like that. I guess I shouldn't have come in to work today. I've been having a touch of flu."

That brought clucks of sympathy and scolding admonitions, quickly followed by plans to see that she got back home immediately to rest. Alex had little to say in the matter. A concerned Jennie drove Alex's car, another agent following to give Jennie a ride back to the office.

Later in the day, Brian Campbell telephoned to inquire if she needed someone to drive her to a doctor or to come over and prepare some food if she was feeling better. She assured him she was much better and would return to work the following day.

"I don't want to see you back in this office the rest of the week," he ordered in a tone that made further arguing futile.

In some ways Alex was grateful for the respite. Even though time hung heavily on her hands, she didn't have to worry about concealing her morning sickness from the eagle gaze of the other women in the office. She slept as late as possible in the mornings and in the afternoons took long walks, trying to sort out her thoughts and decide what to do. She had never before felt so utterly alone in her life, and she avoided seeing anyone, including her parents and good friends like Jinx.

She was torn between a feeling of obligation to her unborn child and love for Vince which made her unwilling to interfere in his life. How could she deny her child the right to know his father? Some uncanny intuition told her she carried a son in her womb. And yet how could she hold Vince responsible for the consequences of her own thoughtless conduct? Honesty coerced her to admit that she alone was to blame for her dilemma. Vince hadn't wanted to have an affair with her—she had all but forced him into it.

The days passed and still she came to no decision. On Sunday evening she contemplated the prospect of returning to work the following day and facing her associates. How could she explain to their satisfaction her rejection of all their offers to visit her and be of help during what they assumed was an ordinary illness? Finally they had even stopped calling to see how she was feeling.

The chime of the doorbell interrupted these troubled reflections, and Alex went reluctantly to answer the door, dreading the prospect of a well-intentioned visitor. Right now she just wanted to be left alone.

"Courtney!" she exclaimed, stunned to see her ex-husband standing outside her door. "What are you doing here?"

"Could I talk to you, Alex? Just for a few minutes—*please*!"

Alex stood and looked at him uncertainly. His pleading air was completely unfamiliar to her, and there wasn't a trace of his usual swaggering, superior attitude. Her own unhappiness made her even more responsive than usual to the needs of another human being, and she opened the door and admitted him.

"What did you want to talk to me about, Courtney?" she asked as she led him from the small foyer into the living room and sat down on the edge of an armchair.

"You haven't heard about my father, have you, Alex?" he asked abruptly. He remained standing and his hands were tensed into fists inside his trouser pockets.

"Your father? Why, no," she said, puzzled.

"I didn't think you had," he interrupted in that same abrupt manner. "We've kept it quiet for business reasons." He paused and Alex could see muscles tightening in his throat as he fought to control his emotion. "He had a massive heart attack two days ago. If he pulls through, he won't be able to do anything for a long time—maybe for the rest of his life."

"Courtney! I *am* sorry to hear that!" Alex's concern and sympathy were genuine, for the elder Jameson had always been kind to her, openly disapproving of his son's cavalier behavior. He had also opposed the divorce right up to the end, making it clear that as far as he was concerned, marriage vows were indissoluble.

"Who's going to take over in your father's place?" Alex's mind had moved ahead to the inevitable question. It wouldn't be easy to find someone to replace a man who ruled single-handedly several large businesses, including one of the main banks in Stokely. Courtney was the only son and major heir, but as a possible successor he had proved a huge disappointment to his father.

"I am," Courtney replied grimly, and met unflinchingly the disbelief in her eyes. "I know what you're thinking, Alex, and I can't blame you. I've been a rotten son—and a rotten husband too. But I want to change that now. And I can—if I get the chance. I *know* I can!"

Incredulity caused Alex to widen her eyes, then a sliver of suspicion entered her mind. "Your father made provisions for something like this happening, didn't he, Courtney? And he didn't leave you in charge."

The affirmative answer was imprinted clearly on his face, which contorted as he struggled to get his emotions under control. "You've *got* to help me, Alex. If I can prove to my father I've really changed—if I can gain his trust and confidence . . . I want to for *his* sake more than mine. You should *see* him now!"

His voice implored her to believe him, and the desperation evident in his whole bearing convinced her of his seriousness in the astounding notion he was proposing. Courtney actually wanted her to marry him again as part of his personal rehabilitation plan.

She could see no reason to question the unselfishness of his motives, for he had been indulged from birth with all that money could buy and there was no likelihood that his personal income would be lessened by his father's invalidhood *or* death, for that matter. She listened quietly as Courtney told her in a voice raw with emotion of how he had comprehended the utter uselessness of his life and was now sorry for having disappointed his parents. He wanted to make up for his failure before it was too late, if it wasn't already.

"I need you, Alex. If you'll come back to me, I swear I'll be a different man."

Her instinctive reaction was to refuse. She wished Courtney no ill will, but the scars he had inflicted couldn't be erased with a sudden about-face and recognition of his errors. Besides—and this was the most important reason not to accept his proposal—she didn't love Courtney and never would: she loved Vince.

But Courtney had unwittingly opened up an avenue of escape from the trap in which she found herself. If she married him again, her child would have a father.

"I'll think about it, Courtney," she promised. "You'll have to give me a little time."

He was visibly relieved by her answer and made a final attempt to strengthen his hand before he left. "Seven years is a lot of time to just write off as a total waste, Alex. And you know your parents, as well as mine, would be glad to see us back together again."

Privately she had to acknowledge the truth of that last statement. Her parents had been wonderfully supportive of her during the separation and divorce but, like Courtney's parents, they came from an old-fashioned tradition and believed in the permanency of marriage bonds. They would indeed be delighted if she went back with Courtney as long as they could be convinced she was acting in her best interests. They wouldn't have been human, either, if they hadn't taken delight in the beautiful house and material possessions that had been hers as Mrs. Courtney Jameson.

By the time she left for work the next morning, struggling in vain to ignore the enervating morning sickness, she had made up her mind to accept Courtney's proposal. As far as she had been able to reason everything out, she would be doing the best she could for everyone involved but herself, and she couldn't help feeling she *deserved* to be unhappy since she had nobody but herself to blame for the mess she had made of her life, beginning with her first marriage to Courtney.

She hadn't yet come to grips with the problem of whether to tell Courtney she was pregnant with another man's child or just allow him to believe it was his own. He would be terribly busy during the next few months trying to prove his capability for taking over the family business interests. He would hardly have time to notice her, and it shouldn't be any problem convincing him the baby was premature if she decided *not* to tell him the truth.

Steeling herself to meet shrewd Brian Campbell, she went straight to his office to tell him her decision to quit her job and remarry her ex-husband. His reaction was so disconcertingly direct she found herself floundering for a reply when he asked gently, "*Why* are you doing this, Alex? You don't look terribly happy over the prospect."

"I'm just tired . . . you *know* I've been sick lately . . . I'm happy, *really* I am." She tried to summon a smile to reassure him and failed dismally in the attempt. "Oh, Brian, I'm truly sorry to let you down like this—after all the money Globe Travel has put into training me . . ." Her voice faltered and she turned her head to avoid his penetrating gaze.

"That has nothing to do with it, Alex," he said quietly, watching her closely. "Why the big hurry? Why don't you just continue working here for a while and give yourself some time to make sure you're making the right decision."

"You don't understand all the circumstances, Brian— and right now I'm not free to tell you." The last was true in more ways than one. Courtney had urged her not to mention to anyone yet the seriousness of his father's condition, and of course she couldn't reveal to Brian her real reason for remarrying.

"Please, just believe me when I say I'm doing the right thing—for everybody . . ." Her agitation at having to avoid answering his questions honestly only increased her queasiness, and she feared she might have to make a dash for the washroom at any moment.

"Go back home, Alex. You don't look well at all." He was observing her pale face with narrowed eyes. "We'll talk later about your quitting your job."

She was in no condition to argue with him. She fled from the room and, ignoring the curious eyes of the agents in the outer office, walked outside to the street, gulping air to calm the waves of nausea.

With the whole day before her, she decided on impulse to drive to Atlanta and consult a physician. Maybe there was something else wrong with her and she wasn't pregnant at all. In a huge city the size of Atlanta, she would be able to find out the truth without taking the risk of publicizing her condition to the whole of Stokely.

Well, at least I know now, she reflected calmly as she drove home hours later in the summer dusk. The doctor's examination had confirmed what she already knew and helped to finalize her decision to marry Courtney again. Resolutely she blocked all other courses of action from her mind.

The following morning she was still lying in bed, succumbing to the morning affliction which Dr. Paine had assured her his prescription would alleviate, when the doorbell chimed. At first Alex decided just to ignore the unwelcome visitor, but whoever it was pressed the button again and again until finally she sighed resignedly and got out of bed.

Not really caring that her hair was uncombed and she probably looked as washed out as she felt, she tied the sash of her robe around her waist and went to answer the door.

"Yes," she said irritably, opening the door a fraction without taking off the safety chain. "Vince! It's *you*!" she gasped, stunned not just at his unexpected presence outside her door but also at his appearance. His face was haggard and showed the dark shadow of an incipient beard. He stood with legs braced apart and shoulders slumped, as if standing upright was a great effort.

Alex fumbled with the chain, finally freeing it, and swung the door open. "Come in," she urged worriedly. "You look *awful*!"

His dark eyes, dull with fatigue, swept over her. "You don't look so hot yourself, Alex," he said wearily. "What's wrong—are you still sick?"

Suddenly remembering what *was* wrong, Alex evaded

the question by asking one of her own as she trailed after him into the living room. "Why are you here?"

Not waiting for an invitation, he dropped down on one end of the low sofa, his long legs sprawled in front of him. "For want of a better excuse, I've come to congratulate you. Forgive my unkempt appearance, but I haven't slept in some time." His voice rang with a bitterness that seemed to cut right through Alex, and a spasm of nausea hit her.

Her knees buckled and she crouched on the edge of a chair set at an angle to the sofa, bending slightly forward and hugging her convulsing abdomen. "Con–congratulate me?" she managed between set teeth.

"I understand from Brian that you've decided to give matrimony another try—with Courtney again. What happened to change your mind, Alex—do you love him?" The harshness of his voice rasped along Alex's nerves, making her wince, but she was helpless to lie. His dark eyes seemed to bore into the recesses of her soul.

"No," she admitted, chewing her lip nervously. His appearance had thrown her completely off guard. She was at a loss to know what to say until she learned why he had come, but before she could ask again, words were spewing out of him like molten rocks from a volcano.

"If it's not the man you want, Alex, then what is it? The social position? The glamour of the Jameson name? It can't be just money. I have as much of that now as Jameson—" He broke off with a deep sigh, as though suddenly wearied beyond endurance with the effort of speaking, and leaned his head back against the sofa, his eyes closed. "Some fools never learn. What rotten luck that I had to be there the day you came into the agency."

Alex felt light-headed suddenly, the thoughts whirling through her brain like autumn leaves in a brisk wind and then settling suddenly into an orderly pattern—that other masculine voice in Brian's office the day she walked into Globe Travel and asked to see the manager, the telephone call that had wrought such a transformation in Brian's manner: Vince had been there in person the whole time! He was responsible for her getting the job!

"*Why*, Vince?" The tiniest flame of hope had ignited inside her at this amazing revelation, and she held her breath waiting for his answer.

"Why?" he echoed mockingly, lifting his head slightly so that he could see her. "I should think that was very obvious to you. I had never managed to get you out of my system—and believe me, I tried." His bitter words brought a vivid image of Gloria Allen to Alex's mind, and she wanted to ask if the rumor about his engagement was true. But she didn't dare interrupt him now.

"I didn't come to Stokely unless it was absolutely necessary to come into the office. I told myself I didn't want to hear anything about you, take the chance of running into you on the street or in a restaurant." His laugh was harsh and self-deprecating, not pleasant to hear. "What a joke! The only reason I opened a branch office in my old home town in the first place was to have the excuse to breathe the same air you breathed."

The raw torment in his voice washed over Alex, making her ache to go over to him, comfort him. But she was prevented from doing that because of the questions he still had not answered.

"Vince . . ." she began hesitantly.

"Don't feel sorry for me, Alex," he interrupted savagely. "I don't need or want your pity."

Alex took a deep breath, one part of her mind noting with relief that her queasiness was beginning to subside. "Why didn't you come out and speak to me that first day—at the agency?"

"I didn't have the nerve," he admitted with heavy irony, observing her now between narrowed lids. "One moment I was deep in conference with Brian—oblivious to your existence—and then suddenly you were right outside the room, in the flesh. I panicked at the thought of seeing you face to face after seven years." He laughed again, bitterly but not as abrasively as before. "Brian was more than a little confused over the whole situation."

"You could hear me talking to Brian, couldn't you?" she prompted, remembering now details of that day which had wrought such sweeping change in her life.

He nodded. "I could hear you. There was something scared and uncertain underneath the assertiveness. I acted without even thinking when I heard Brian about to turn you down—picked up the phone and ordered him to take your application." He was composed now, speaking quietly as though he had reached deep inside to tap some reservoir of strength. "We didn't have an opening at the time, and I was breaking all precedent interfering as I did to create a position, going over the branch manager's head. And ordinarily, of course, we wouldn't think of sending a novice off to a foreign country—"

"Nor does the owner of the company personally train a new employee," Alex interposed dryly, shaking her head to her own former naïveté. Everything was suddenly so clear, including the restraint in the attitudes of the other agents in the office. "I still don't understand why you went to so much trouble and expense, when—"

"When all I would have had to do was walk out of Brian Campbell's office that day. Or pick up the telephone and call you at home later. I had my reasons, even though they may not be the most admirable." He shook his head ruefully. "I wanted to meet you on entirely different territory this time—where I would have the upper hand."

"But you were so completely honorable!" Alex protested, remembering the two weeks in Portugal and his impeccable behavior. "I was the one who eventually had to seduce you!"

"That's only because I took one look at you that night in the lobby at the Hotel Jorge and found myself standing in the same shoes—seven years later. I was scared to breathe, to do anything that might send you rushing back to Stokely and out of my life again. You made it painfully clear you were turned off by the idea of remarrying and giving up your freedom. I was too big a coward to make love to you because . . ." His voice had grown hoarse and strained, as if the words caused him considerable pain. ". . . I knew it would really be hell after that to give you up. And I was right . . ."

"But that night at the casino, our last night together in Portugal, and the next day on the plane, you acted so cold and strange," she reminded him, color returning to her cheeks now. The nausea had disappeared completely and joyous hope was pumping through her veins.

"Self-defense," he explained wearily, running restless fingers through his hair. "You were like a beautiful bird out of a cage, all poised for flight and dying to try out your wings. My only hope was that you wouldn't find someone else, and when you were ready to settle down— Oh hell, what's the use now? You're going back to Courtney. I've got to catch a plane."

He moved so swiftly he was at the door with his hand on the knob before Alex could catch up with him. "Wait, Vince—*please!*" she begged, grasping his jacket.

"I've got to get out of here, Alex," he said in a low, strangled voice. "I'm human. I can take just so much—"

"Before you go . . . the offer you made that day at the airport . . . if it's still open, I accept," she said breathlessly and waited anxiously as he turned slowly to face her, his dark eyes searching her face.

"I told you, Alex, I don't need your pity," he said coldly.

"I'm not offering you pity, Vince," she answered quickly and saw a look of uncertainty in his eyes. "When I first realized I was in love with you, I knew I could never marry you because I couldn't give you children." She raised her hand against his stifled exclamation. "Please—hear me out. Then I got back here and had good reason to believe I'm not sterile, but I was afraid you might feel sorry for me and insist on marrying me out of a sense of duty—"

Her voice broke off as Vince grasped her by the shoulders and shook her hard. "What are you telling me, Alex?" he demanded, staring down at her face.

"Please don't do that," she breathed, pressing both hands against her abdomen.

He watched the movement intently and then took his hands from her shoulders and thrust them into his pockets. "Are you telling me you're pregnant with my child?" he asked in a strange voice.

"Either that or I have a virus that affects me only in the mornings," she wisecracked in an unsuccessful effort to lighten the tense atmosphere. "Actually I didn't know for sure until yesterday afternoon. I drove to Atlanta to see a doctor—it's a little embarrassing under the circumstances to go to one here in Stokely."

He wheeled away from her and took several steps back toward the living room. When he turned around to face her, she saw the struggle for control mirrored in his features. "You are pregnant with *my* child and yet you were planning to marry Jameson?"

"Please, *please*, Vince, let me explain," she begged.

"I'm listening," he said tersely, and his eyes swept over her trembling form. "You'd better sit down."

They returned to the living room, where Alex took her former position while Vince remained standing, his eyes not leaving her face as she tried to explain to him all the doubts and confusion that had led her to decide to go back to Courtney. She told him of Courtney's visit, his determination to prove to his ill father he was capable of assuming his responsibility, his urgent proposal of marriage and promise to be a better husband this time.

"But none of that was the *real* reason I decided to marry him again, Vince. You had told me yourself in Portugal that you were seriously involved with someone. And then I saw the picture of you and Gloria in a magazine—I hadn't heard a word from you, and I thought . . ."

His face was chiseled stone, his voice as polite as that of a stranger inquiring the time of day when he asked, "Did you plan to *tell* Jameson you were carrying my child, or did you intend to let him believe it was his own?"

"I don't know," she whispered, feeling like someone who had just confessed to a crime punishable by death.

Suddenly she could no longer bear the penetrating scrutiny of his eyes, which burned like live coals in the ashen mask of his face. She put up her hands over her face to avoid those eyes, and tears slid down between her fingers and dropped to form dark spots on the copper-colored fabric of her robe.

"I'm sorry, Vince. I never meant to hurt you again, you've got to believe that," she said brokenly. "I'll understand if you want to leave now. No one ever has to know—"

She jumped convulsively at the unrestrained savagery of his curse, lowering her hands to stare at him, mindless of her tear-streaked countenance. "Let's get one thing straight right now, Alex. No one except me is going to be the father of my child. You're going to marry me, not Jameson."

Those words spoken in a different tone would have made Alex the happiest woman in the world. Instead, she felt as if someone were tolling a bell of doom as she gazed across an unbreachable chasm at the man she loved. His anger had calmed, but deep in his eyes was a hurt she might never be able to heal. This time she didn't have the excuse of youth.

Chapter Nine

"WHERE ARE YOU GOING?"

Alex was finally able to find her voice as Vince turned and walked tiredly toward the foyer. She sounded as unsure as she felt, fearful that he might still be leaving town immediately, as he had been about to do before she stopped him with the bombshell of her pregnancy. She desperately wanted him to stay so that she could convince him she really loved him, in spite of the damning evidence to the contrary.

"To a motel. I have a taxi waiting outside." Without stopping, he spoke these words over his shoulder, his head only half turned so that he couldn't see Alex, who had risen from her chair and was staring after him.

"You could stay here," she offered quickly, and tensed for his reaction as he stopped.

"I'm dead on my feet. The last twenty-four hours have

been pure hell. Ever since Brian called with the news. . . . I'll call you later, after I've gotten a few hours sleep."

He hadn't even turned around, she noted despairingly, watching him disappear through the archway and hearing a few seconds later the sound of the door opening and closing. Probably he couldn't bear the sight of her. He had spoken in the heavy monotone of one who has lost all hope.

Alex sighed deeply, wanting nothing more at the moment than to succumb to the aching frustration welling inside her as she contemplated the thorough mess she had once again made of her life—and Vince's. But then he *had* said he had never gotten over her all those years, and he hadn't confirmed that rumor of an engagement to Gloria Allen. Maybe there was hope for undoing the damage she had done. Maybe he could love her again.

The thought of seeing him later in the day, when he would have had a chance to get some sleep and perhaps would have a less grim perspective, cheered her. She went into the kitchen and made herself some buttered toast and poured out a glass of milk, her morning sickness completely gone now. For the next eight months, she had more than herself to consider: there was the baby to think of, her and Vince's baby.

As she rinsed her dishes and stacked them in the dishwasher and restored the small kitchen to perfect order, Alex found herself humming. Knowing that she and Vince were going to be married, and that their baby would have a secure home, she couldn't remain depressed. Now that she had shared with Vince the news of her pregnancy, it no longer seemed the heavy burden she had carried all alone the past week.

Happier than she had been in weeks, she cleaned the apartment throughly, never openly admitting to herself the reason: she nurtured the hope that Vince would relent and stay there with her rather than at the motel. They were as good as married, and she was unconcerned about the risk of incurring gossip among the tenants of the building.

When the apartment was immaculate, Alex soaked in a tub fragrant with her favorite bath scent. She planned to look ravishing when Vince next saw her. That morning she had looked like a witch and she hoped to erase that memory. It wouldn't do for Vince to think he was marrying a hag.

That afternoon, when she put the finishing touches to her make-up, she knew she had never looked better. Her skin glowed from the facial she had given herself, and her tawny hair fell in lustrous waves almost to her shoulders. The teal-blue jumpsuit she wore flattered the sensuous curves of her slender figure and would be appropriate for dining out in any restaurant in Stokely, if Vince preferred to go out. In the event he might want to eat at the apartment, she had taken steaks from the freezer and had on hand frozen vegetables and salad ingredients. She was prepared for any eventuality—or so she thought.

When the telephone rang at a little past seven, she was beginning to get restless from waiting to hear from Vince and to fret that she hadn't asked the name of the motel where he would be staying. Perhaps, she had begun to reason anxiously, he had forgotten to leave a wake-up call request with the desk clerk.

"Hello," she said eagerly into the telephone receiver, certain the caller was Vince.

"Hello, Alex. Would it be all right if I come over? I need to talk to you." It was Courtney's voice, not Vince's, and it sounded strained and anxious. She had forgotten all about Courtney, who would be wanting to know her decision, whether she had decided to accept his proposal of marriage.

Struggling not to sound as impatient as she felt, Alex spoke firmly into the receiver. "Courtney, I can't invite you here tonight. In fact, it would be better if we didn't meet in person at all. You see, I'm involved with someone else—I'm planning to marry him."

"Why the hell didn't you—"

Alex really couldn't blame Courtney for the shocked and accusative nature of his reply, which was liberally laced with expletives. This was the old Courtney to whom she had been married, not the subdued, cajoling person who had called on her two evenings ago. It eased her conscience to know he hadn't changed so drastically after all. After his first few words, she only half listened to him, impatient to hang up so that the line wouldn't be busy when Vince called.

"Courtney—" she broke in as he switched abruptly from abuse to pleading, "—I'm expecting an important call. I'm sorry, I can't stay on the phone with you any longer." And with those words, she hung up.

The phone rang again seconds later and to her relief it was not Courtney calling again, as she had feared. Vince announced tersely that he would be at her apartment in fifteen minutes, then hung up before she could offer to pick him up in her car. Had she been thinking clearly earlier, she would have offered it to him then.

Fifteen minutes later the doorbell pealed and she hurried to open the door, nervous now that after all her waiting he was here and she would be able to see for herself if he was still angry with her. Her heart stopped momentarily when she saw him standing outside, tall and ruggedly masculine and very stern in a freshly pressed dark suit. He appeared considerably more rested than he had earlier, but his dark eyes were somber as he looked her over, and there was something indomitable in the set of his mouth.

Combatting a rising feeling of foreboding, Alex mustered a big smile as she swung open the door and then preceded him into the living room.

"Can I fix you a drink?" she offered lightly, determined not to give in to the grimness of his countenance.

"Thank you. I'll have a Scotch on ice, if you have Scotch."

Her smile wavered at the chilling politeness of his tone and the memory of the last time she had seen him drink Scotch, that nightmarish final evening in Portugal when he had seemed bent on consuming the world's supply of Scotch.

Without giving voice to her dismay, she turned away toward the sideboard, where she stored her supply of liquor. Earlier she had filled the sterling ice bucket, which had been a wedding present, and placed it along with two glasses on the sideboard. Just as she was reaching for the bottle of Scotch, the doorbell rang, causing her to jump since the sound was so unexpected.

"Expecting somebody?" Vince asked.

"No—nobody," she said, half turning toward him, a line of puzzlement cutting between her eyebrows.

"I'll see who it is," he said brusquely and strode toward the foyer without waiting for her assent.

Alex stood exactly as she was, listening. Before she heard the voice, it came to her in a flash of premonition who the caller was likely to be.

"I want to see Alex."

It was Courtney, just as she had feared. The arrogance in his tone was guaranteed to raise Vince's hackles at any time, but especially in his present mood.

"Sorry. She's busy." Vince's curt voice made it clear he was not sorry.

"Who are *you*, anyway?" Courtney demanded angrily. "If you'll just stand out of my way, I intend to see my wife."

"She is no longer your wife. In a very short time she will be *my* wife, and if you know what's good for you, you won't bother her again."

Alex shivered at the icy steel in Vince's tone and winced at the sharp slam of the door. How unfortunate that Courtney had completely ignored her wishes and turned up here tonight. The incident had served to answer one of her questions, though. In spite of Vince's rigidly controlled exterior, a cauldron of hot anger smoldered inside him. She had wondered if he had begun to forgive her. Now she strongly doubted it.

As he came back into the room, she busied herself pouring Scotch into his glass and then made herself a weak rum and soda.

"Here you are."

A husky tremor betrayed her uneasiness as she approached Vince and handed him the drink. Flinching under the black fury of his dark gaze, she protested, "I *told* him not to come here tonight, Vince. He called a little earlier and asked if he could talk to me. I suppose he hoped he could change my mind..." Alex detested the defensive note in her voice. Then a thought occurred. "I almost got the impression you might have recognized Courtney—even before he said anything," she said hesitantly. "I can't remember the two of you ever meeting."

"I recognized him," Vince replied curtly, his tone and forbidding countenance discouraging pursuit of the topic, or indeed conversation on any subject.

They finished their drinks with a minimum of conversation and then left the apartment to go out to dinner at a quiet restaurant reputed to be the best steakhouse in town, though not the fanciest in décor. Vince had peremptorily refused Alex's timid offer to cook dinner for the two of them.

To her relief he did not have another Scotch before dinner, ordering a bottle of wine instead from the very limited selection. Alex had one glass but turned down a refill, explaining with a touch of shyness, "I don't want to get Junior here intoxicated." She rubbed her flat stomach. "Did I tell you I have this strong hunch it's a boy?"

Vince had been staring at the motion of her hand and looked up to her face with a strange expression, a spasm of emotion quivering across his features, but he did not reply. During the entire meal he said almost nothing, seeming to be absorbed in eating and pondering his own private thoughts. Only after the waitress had cleared away their plates and set steaming cups of coffee in front of them did he break the silence and bring up the subject of their marriage.

"Under the circumstances, there won't be time for a lot of fuss and preparation," he warned.

"I don't mind," she assured him eagerly. "I went through all that when Courtney and I—" She broke off, regretting she had brought up the subject of her first marriage when she saw Vince's features settle into an iron mask. Watching him as he stared down into his cup, Alex felt a shaft of despair knife into her chest. Would it always be like this between her and Vince? From time to time it was inevitable that she would make some innocent reference to the past, as she had done just now. Her whole point had been to reassure Vince that she didn't care about a fancy wedding, that she didn't think it important in promoting happiness between two people.

"Where will we live?" she asked, changing the subject.

His dark eyes lifted to meet hers, their expression guarded. "Unless you wish otherwise, here in Stokely." He hesitated for a brief moment. "My work requires a great deal of travel, as you already know. I'll feel better if you are close to family and friends."

Alex's heart plummeted like a heavy boulder heaved into the sea. Her common sense told her a man in Vince's position, at the top of a successful corporation, could curtail his business travel if he wanted to. Globe Travel must have any number of well-trained and ambitious men eager to take over some of his duties. She knew the real truth—Vince wanted an excuse to be away from Stokely or, more precisely, to be away from *her*.

The bright optimism which had buoyed her spirits all that afternoon began to ebb as a new fear was born in her heart. Did Vince intend them to have a real marriage, or was it just to be an empty facade for the benefit of the outside world to legitimize their child? She didn't have the courage to ask him outright for fear the answer would be more than she could bear just now.

"If you agree, then, it's settled. We'll start looking for a house to buy here in Stokely." Vince stood up, as if finalizing the decision.

The ride back to Alex's apartment was a quiet one. She started once to suggest he use her car to drive back to his motel rather than have to rely on a taxi, but bit back the words, resolving to put aside her pride once they had arrived at the apartment. She would offer again to let him share the apartment with her during the next few days before they were married. He might spurn the offer, but she had to try to close the gap between them.

All evening she had been yearning to feel his arms around her, enclosing her in their strength and tenderness. Now in the darkness of the car, she allowed herself to recapture the magic of his love-making, shivering involuntarily at the memory of his lips demanding and passionate against hers, his strong, wonderful hands stroking and molding all her pliant curves. How she longed to have him awaken once again all the nerves and fibers of her body as he had done during those few precious days together in Portugal. If he would put aside his pride and resentment, they could enjoy again the marvelous joining of their bodies.

Inflamed by these thoughts, Alex walked beside Vince up the open flight of steps and down the breezeway to the door of her apartment, holding her breath in suspense. He held out his hand for her key, took it, and thrust it into the lock. With a deft twist of his hand, he had the door unlocked and pushed it open.

"Are you coming in?" The acceleration of her heartbeat made the blood pulse in her ears so she had to strain to hear his answer.

"No. I'll go on back to the motel."

He loomed so tall and unapproachable as he stood looking down at her, his face in shadow, that she quaked inwardly and had to conduct a desperate search for the remnants of her courage. Only the thought of going inside the apartment alone, without him, while he went to some impersonal motel room bolstered her flagging initiative. Reaching up and placing her hands on his shoulders, she tried not to notice that he seemed to recoil under her touch.

"Vince, I love you," she said softly. "Please, won't you stay with me?"

Her plea met with leaden silence. To her heightened fancy, his shoulders tensed to coils of steel under her palms.

"There's one thing I've been wondering, Alex." His voice, harsh and rasping, scraped painfully against her already tautened nerves. "Did you intend to sleep with him?"

Speechless, she stared up into his face, which was contorted by savage scorn. She moved her head slowly from side to side, as if in disbelief, bit her trembling lower lip, but she was unable to speak. A great numbing hopelessness invaded the yawning emptiness inside her, making words seem pitifully ineffectual in the face of his withering accusation. What could she answer? In truth, she hadn't thought that far when she was planning to remarry Courtney; the sexual part of marriage had been the furthest consideration from her mind.

"I think I have the answer to my question. You've answered it by not answering—and you expect me to believe you love me." Vince's laugh, harsh and bitter, was like a file scraping away the sensitive outer covering of her heart. She whimpered in pain like a helpless puppy trod underfoot, but he didn't hear because he had already turned and now strode away from her, soon disappearing down the steps and out into the darkness.

"He should have taken the car," she whispered brokenly, staring after him long after he was no longer in sight. Finally, she mustered the energy to go inside. She stood for a while leaning against the closed door, feeling utterly lifeless and numb. It was very quiet. She could feel her aching loneliness, and it was her only company for the night.

Alex slept the sleep of the emotionally exhausted and awoke with the vaguely disturbing awareness that something was wrong. In seconds she remembered everything, and the resulting mental turmoil seemed to intensify the curious heaviness and nausea which afflicted her each morning, destroying all her normal initiative to get out of bed. She lay there, miserable and ill.

When the doorbell sounded, penetrating the thick fog of her lethargy, she groaned aloud and muttered, "Go away. Leave me alone." She knew it had to be Vince, and she couldn't bear to face him now. She shuddered to have him see her like this, at her worst. If she didn't answer the door, surely he would leave and go somewhere to telephone her. Later in the day, when she had recovered both physically and mentally, she would welcome him.

After several pealing summonses, the doorbell finally rang no more. Assuming that her prediction of his actions must be accurate, Alex relaxed her rigid muscles, turning over on one side and curling her body into the fetal position, her head burrowed into the pillow and the sheet pulled up to cover her eyes.

She must have drifted back to sleep, secure in the belief that she had kept in abeyance for a few more hours the necessity of facing reality, for she did not hear the sound of a key turning in the lock of her apartment door. Nor was she aware of the presence of another person until she was startled awake by the lifting of the sheet away from her face. Her eyes flew open in mindless panic, and she looked up into Vince's face. Her first thought was to wonder why he looked so deeply worried. And how had he gotten into her apartment?

"How—" she began confusedly.

"I got the key from your manager," he explained briefly.

Feeling unbearably vulnerable with him standing over her, Alex turned over on her other side, presenting him with her back. Judging from the expression on his face, she thought she must look even more ghastly than she had feared.

"What time is it?" she muttered into her pillow, just for something to say while she tried to collect her poise.

"Nine-thirty. . . . Why didn't you answer when I rang the doorbell? Are you too ill to get out of bed?" Alex could tell from his voice that he was torn between alarm and vexation. As an only child and a bachelor, he probably knew very little about the morning sickness that accompanies the early stage of pregnancy.

"I'm sorry. I didn't mean to upset you. It's just that I feel so *awful* . . . and I look like a witch. It passes after a while." God, here she was first thing in the morning apologizing to him again. Would she ever do anything *right* where he was concerned?

"Isn't there something you can take for it—some medicine a doctor could prescribe?"

Alex rolled over on her back, forgetting that she didn't want him to see her looking so wan and pale. "I forgot all about the prescription Dr. Paine gave me. I meant to have it filled yesterday, but then you showed up and I didn't give it a thought."

"Where is it?"

"In my handbag, over there on the dresser."

She watched him as he went over to the dresser, opened her leather handbag, and found the prescription, giving it just a cursory glance before tucking it into an inside breast pocket. The lightweight tan suit he wore was superbly tailored to his tall length, suggesting his lean fitness. His dark hair was thick and vital, neatly styled but somehow not completely tamed. Alex wasn't too ill to feel a stir of pleasure at his masculine good looks.

"I'll be back as soon as I have this filled—no, don't get out of bed. Stay there." The latter was in response

to her movement to get up. She had sat up, the sheet
falling away unheeded around her hips. It was only when
Vince's dark eyes flicked over her, their expression suddenly more intent, that she remembered she wore a
skimpy nightgown whose lace insets concealed little of
the inviting curves of her breasts. Without drawing up
the sheet to cover her, she lay back on the pillow as he
had ordered.

"Okay," she said meekly.

After he had gone, she disobeyed him immediately,
getting out of bed and going into the bathroom to wash
her face and brush her hair into glossy order. Before
climbing back into bed, she plumped the pillows and
smoothed the bedcovers. Her morning sickness had not
dissipated altogether, but she felt immeasurably cheered
by Vince's presence. He emanated a quiet, dependable
strength that eased her anxieties and revitalized her hope
that matters would work out for them. Somehow she
would prove her love to him and make up for the hurt
she had caused him. In time he would grow to trust her.
Until then, the intimacy of the bedroom was as good a
place as any to begin building the closeness a good marriage should have. Vince was not indifferent to her sex-
ually, that much she knew from the expression in his
eyes a few minutes ago as they lingered on the tempting
fullness of her breasts.

Preoccupied with these optimistic reflections, Alex
lay and waited for Vince to return. The sound of the door
opening and closing brought a thrill of happiness as she
contemplated a future in which she shared the same living
quarters with this very special man whom she adored
with all her heart and soul.

"Welcome back!" she called out gaily.

He entered the bedroom shortly, carrying a bottle of
pills and a glass of water. He set them down on the table
beside her bed, his eyes devoid of expression as he took
in at a glance the straightened bed and the gleaming
honey softness of her hair. Yet he made no mention of

the evidence that she had disobeyed his instructions and gotten out of bed, nor did he reveal any appreciation of the smooth expanse of neck and shoulders bared by the narrow straps of the gown. As he spoke he allowed his gaze to drift no lower than her face, which was regaining its normal, healthy color.

"Take one of these. I'll check back in a few hours and see if you're feeling up to lunch. This afternoon we'll apply for the license and do whatever else is required. Your parents have to be told too." He spoke in a calm, matter-of-fact voice, as if he were working out the mundane details of a business contract. Then he turned away and headed for the door without a word of conventional sympathy or even a goodbye.

Alex was both disappointed and annoyed. "Where are you going?" she demanded and then flushed under his gaze as he swung around, his eyebrows raised in sardonic questioning at her tone.

"Sorry," she murmured, averting her eyes from his. "I didn't mean to sound like a nagging wife."

Ignoring the rueful apology, he explained in a detached, formal voice his plans for the morning. "I need to drop by the office and talk to Brian. While I'm there, I'll make some telephone calls and rearrange my schedule for the next few days—until after we're married and you're settled."

Alex stared after his back as he left. He couldn't have made it any plainer that once they were married he would resume his normal business schedule, which meant he would probably be traveling most of the time. Finally it was beginning to dawn on her that Vince had no intention of putting aside the past as she had hoped he would do. He never really had, not even in Portugal, when she had felt there was a barrier between them. In Sintra, when she had acted so impulsively, her main purpose had been to tear down the wall separating her from Vince. Ultimately she had failed, for although Vince had allowed himself to be tricked into making love to her, their physical intimacy had not given her entry into the corridors of his private soul. Plainly he had no intention of letting her gain such access even after they were married.

The sobering insights of that morning proved all too true in the next few days. Alex found herself almost constantly in Vince's company, but she made no inroads into his cool detachment. The courtesy of his manner toward her was unimpeachable, and there seemed to be no trace of a churlish grudge, no further reference to the betrayal he felt from her desperate plan to remarry Courtney. But at times it was all Alex could do to restrain an outburst of frustration as she failed repeatedly in her efforts to establish some basis for understanding between them.

They were married by a minister in her parents' living room with only her mother and father present. Afterward, the four of them went out to dinner at Stokely's most elegant restaurant, which happened to be located in the same luxury motel in which Vince was staying. It was during the meal that Alex learned that her new husband did not, as she had assumed, plan to move into the apartment with her until they found a house to buy.

"I hope you'll find something soon," Alex's mother sympathized. "It's too bad your apartment is so small, Alex." Her face took on a thoughtful expression, as if she were visualizing the apartment. "There isn't even an extra bedroom for Vince to use as a study. But maybe you could just rent a larger apartment until you find exactly what you want in a house." Brightening on this note, she looked questioningly at her daughter and her new son-in-law.

Vince's expression was unreadable. "You'd probably be amazed how many houses are for sale in Stokely, considering this isn't really what you'd call a transient area. I'm confident we'll find something right away." He sipped from his water glass. "In the meantime, I'll just keep the suite I have here to use as an office."

Alex's eyes flew to meet his, sickened by the message she read in their dark, implacable depths. He didn't intend to use the suite just as an office, but as his sleeping quarters too. She should have known he would not subject himself to the close proximity that living with her in the apartment would force upon them. And she, poor fool, had been counting the days until the wedding, telling herself Vince would not be able to maintain his present cold distance when the two of them were forced to share her bedroom with its double bed.

During the remainder of the dinner, she was aware now and then of circumspect glances from her parents, who had received the news of her sudden wedding plans with admirable stoicism and the minimum of curiosity. They knew, of course, that she was pregnant, but they didn't know that the relationship between her and Vince was anything but normal. For their sakes, Alex would have acted like a happy bride if doing so had been within her power, if she weren't plagued with a heavy, aching mass in the place where her heart was supposed to be. Under the circumstances she did the best she could, but the results were not convincing, even to her.

During the following days, she found that nothing had changed to soften Vince toward her. He turned all his energies to finding a house and she knew the reason for his urgency: he wanted to get her settled so that he would be free to leave.

With that knowledge constantly in her mind, she found herself hoping they wouldn't find anything to please him. As much as she dreamed of making a wonderful home for the two of them and the child she was carrying, she couldn't bear to think of being alone again. As unsatisfactory as their present living arrangement was, she had at least a little piece of him, his physical presence. It was better than the alternative—nothing.

Several times they looked at houses Alex liked, but each time she found faults, finally drawing a questioning gaze from Vince for the flimsiness of some of her criticisms. But whatever his private thoughts on her inability to find a house to satisfy all her requirements, he said nothing. Then unwittingly she gave him a glimpse into her true taste.

One afternoon when they had traipsed through five or six houses and had given up for the day, they were driving back to her apartment, passing through the oldest residential area in Stokely, the houses all stately and beautifully maintained, set far back from the street on immaculate grounds. The real-estate sign in front of a lovely two-story blue-gray house with white shutters brought an exclamation of surprise from Alex.

"The Pennington house is for sale! When I was in high school, I went to a party there and felt like Cinderella at the ball." She was quiet then, remembering the occasion. She hadn't been invited by Sally Pennington, who was a year older than Alex and not too friendly toward those she considered her social inferiors, which included a good portion of Stokely's citizens. Alex had gone as the date of a boy who lived in the same exclusive neighborhood.

"Why don't we look at it tomorrow morning?" Vince's quiet voice cut into her reminiscence.

Alex's hazel eyes mirrored her astonishment. "Do you have any idea what a house in this neighborhood would cost? Besides, it's huge."

Anger flared up in Vince's eyes as they connected with hers. "What does it matter how much it costs? I can afford any house in this town. When did I give you a ceiling price? I've been wondering—" His terse voice broke off, and he stared ahead through the windshield, his jawline ridged with tense muscles.

Alex knew what he had been wondering: why she had consistently chosen to look at houses that were not large or expensive? Vince had never mentioned any price category, and she hadn't wanted to seem mercenary and acquisitive. Besides, she had good reason to suspect she would be the sole occupant most of the time, once she was settled in. The larger the house, the more room she would have to be lonely in it.

"I'm sorry, Vince," she said in a low, miserable voice, which deepened into bitterness. "That's all I ever seem to be able to say to you—*I'm sorry, Vince.*"

"It's not entirely your fault. I should have guessed—and said something."

She knew the words hadn't been easy for him to say: they sounded as though they had been wrenched from him. But with them spoken Alex felt they were in a state of truce, and she sought to undo some damage by explaining her feelings. He listened, but disappointingly he didn't refute her theory that she would be spending a lot of time alone in their future house.

The next morning they looked through the Pennington house, accompanied by yet another zealous real-estate agent. It was even lovelier than Alex remembered, the large, high-ceilinged rooms having a grace and dignity she loved. In her mind she was arranging furniture and selecting drapery material the whole time she accompanied Vince and the agent from room to room. When the tour was completed, she preceded the two men out onto the brick front walk, content to have Vince handle the agent's inevitable sales pitch: a house like this wouldn't be long on the market; if they liked it, they might want to sign a purchase contract right away; he had one with him in his briefcase in the car. It was a familiar routine to her by now, having looked at so many houses in the company of eager agents.

"Do you think your clients would be open to an offer?" Hearing Vince's deep voice took Alex completely by surprise. He hadn't even consulted her! She had fallen in love with the house on sight, but how did he *know* that?

Chapter Ten

"I JUST CAN'T believe this is really *ours*!" Alex exclaimed a few days later as Vince parked in the driveway of their new house.

The transaction was complete except for the necessary title work, and in the meantime the former owners had given their permission for Alex to begin furnishing and decorating the house. She had suggested rather tentatively to Vince that perhaps they should furnish just the basic rooms they would need and leave the others to a later time, but he had firmly overruled that idea, leaving no margin for misunderstanding as to his wishes.

"I've opened an account for you to draw on. I want you to spend all of it and more too, if you need it." He mentioned a sum that made her gasp. She had been wondering if he realized how expensive it would be to furnish a house that large with furniture befitting its age and beauty, not to mention the cost of custom draperies, area rugs, and accessories. Evidently, he did realize.

Several other questions had been plaguing Alex too, but she didn't know quite how to introduce them since they were of such a sensitive nature. It was while she was looking through the upstairs rooms with Vince, deciding on alterations or repairs which should be taken care of immediately, that she seized her opportunity to hint at one question.

"I think this is the nicest bedroom, don't you?" she asked, standing in the door of a large corner room with windows facing south and east so that it would receive early morning sun and yet be spared the punishing rays of the afternoon.

"You take that one, then. I'll take this one." He walked over to the room next to the one she had indicated.

Alex sagged against the door frame, teeth sinking painfully into her lower lip. She had her answer without even asking the question that had been nagging at her. It shouldn't have come as any surprise that Vince had no intention of sharing a bedroom with her. At least he would be in the same house now, she reflected bitterly, and not across town in a motel.

"I hope you don't object to sharing the bathroom," she said when she had recovered enough from her disappointment to speak. It was impossible to hold back the undertone of bitter sarcasm.

Vince ignored her tone, moving across the hall to gaze into an old-fashioned bathroom as large as a bedroom in many modern houses. "Are you planning to replace the old fixtures with new ones?"

"Heavens, no!" Alex exclaimed in genuine horror, coming to stand beside him. "That's a part of its charm. Some new tile and new wallpaper..." As she outlined her ideas for the bathroom, the subject of separate bedrooms temporarily forgotten, her face glowed with enthusiasm, her natural beauty heightened by her animation.

Aware of the intentness of Vince's scrutiny of her features, Alex interpreted it as absorption in what she was telling him. Consequently, she was quite taken aback when she stopped to ask his opinion in the choice of colors and was rewarded by a blank expression. Hadn't he been listening to what she said?

"I have complete confidence in your taste," he said noncommittally after a second of awkwardness. "Personally, I'm more concerned about the soundness of the plumbing."

They had gone through the entire house, Alex jotting notes so that later she wouldn't forget any of the things that had to be attended to, when Vince answered another of the questions she had been too timid to introduce, fearful of evoking painful associations. As it turned out, her caution had been well founded.

Much of what she was using in the apartment had belonged to her and Courtney when they were married: her silver and china and crystal, all of which were of considerable value, plus many items of furniture and accessories. Most of it could be adapted to use, even if only temporarily, in her new home. But thus far she hadn't had the nerve to ask Vince if he objected.

"How long do you estimate it will take to get the place ready to move in?" he asked as they were about to leave the house.

Alex stopped to consider. "That all depends on what you mean by *ready*. As soon as the messy work like the painting and repapering are finished, and these things are taken care of," she waved the tablet in her hand, "we could go ahead and live here while the rest is being done. We can move my things from the apartment—"

She broke off in the middle of the tentative suggestion when she saw anger blaze up in his dark eyes, igniting them into an inferno of contempt. The tanned skin of his face was stretched taut across his strong bone structure, and his finely modeled mouth was twisted into a snarl. Alex flinched before the barely controlled violence of his words, which spewed out like fragments of red-hot steel.

"I won't have *anything* Courtney Jameson owned or even *touched* in my house—*our* house. You can do whatever you please with that stuff in your apartment—sell it, donate it to charity, *give* it away! I don't care one way or the other—but don't bring a single piece of it here."

Alex felt as if her face had been ravaged by a blazing forest fire when Vince finally turned away from her, walking a few steps away and standing with his hands clenched into fists and his tall frame rigid with the struggle to harness the anger raging inside him. She was deeply shaken at the resurfacing of this violent emotion after days when he had seemed perfectly calm. Lulled into believing his terrible anger at her had cooled, she had proof once again that it smoldered dangerously inside him, ready to ignite at a careless spark.

The practical side of her nature protested at what seemed needless expense to purchase new everything they would require for day-to-day living, not to mention elegant entertaining. But she didn't dare mention that pragmatic aspect of what Vince was ordering her to do. If she did, she might unleash the rage he was fighting to control. While she knew intuitively he would never do physical harm to her, she couldn't bear to have him suffer the searing pain she saw in his dark eyes, in the contortion of his strong features and the aching rigidity of his long frame. These spurts of anger were like brief seizures lasting only seconds but devastating in their destructive intensity.

Facing him across the table at lunch an hour later, Alex found it incredible that this calm, imperturbable man was the same one who had trembled with rage before her a short time earlier. His manner was remote as he inquired of her immediate plans for beginning the work on the house. Something in the wording of his questions and comments raised an alarm in Alex's head. Her emotional antennae quivered and alerted her that what she had been dreading was about to happen: Vince was leaving Stokely. The flash of premonition did not make the impact of his announcement any less painful, especially when she learned how soon he intended to depart.

"I have to catch a plane to New York this afternoon," he mentioned casually.

"This afternoon!" she echoed, paling. "But why didn't you *tell* me—"

"I just found out about it myself this morning. It's something I really must attend to personally." His tone was even, his dark eyes veiled, and Alex knew with a pang of helplessness there was nothing she could say or do to persuade him to stay. Whether the business had come up unexpectedly and was urgent, as he would have her believe, she had no way of knowing. What saddened and dismayed her, though, was the intuition which told her he would not return for a long time.

He had married her, bought her one of Stokely's finest old houses, and was providing her with almost unlimited funds to furnish and decorate it, but he refused to give her what she really wanted: himself—his love, his companionship, his trust. All these were denied her. She would have to take solace in creating for him a beautiful home with the hope that in time he would want to share it with her and their child.

Overriding his objections, Alex drove Vince to the Atlanta airport and accompanied him all the way to the waiting room outside the gate. When the first call for boarding the airplane resounded over the speakers, Vince arose immediately from his chair beside her.

"Take care of yourself. I'll be calling to check on you and the progress on the house."

Alex felt a tearing sensation in her chest and the sting of tears behind her eyelids. Was he really going to walk away from her with just those stiff words of parting as though they were nothing to each other? She was his wife, carrying his child inside her womb. Did that mean nothing to him?

"Aren't you even going to kiss me goodbye?" she asked unsteadily, all pride gone at the devastating prospect of having him out of her life for an indeterminate amount of time. Through the blur of her tears she saw him tense and stare down at her. Slowly, he bent his head toward her and placed his lips against hers. She felt them cool and firm and passive against the quivering softness of hers. A low pleading sound came from her throat, and she reached up and grasped his head, holding him there, begging him mutely for something more. His mouth moved gently against hers then, and she savored the poignant sweetness of the kiss, big wet tears rolling down her cheeks and adding their saltiness to the taste of his lips.

Still clasping his head, she parted her lips invitingly, offering and imploring him to deepen the tender kiss into passion. His arms moved jerkily as if struggling to free themselves from an invisible cord binding them to his side. Succeeding, they closed around her, crushing her against him. At the same time his mouth began to devour hers with a fierce, urgent hunger that awoke the song of desire in her bloodstream and dissolved her bones so that she had to cling helplessly to him, answering the demand of his kiss with a need that matched his own. His hands moved along her spine, hungry for the feel of her. His tongue plundered the willing sweetness of her mouth. The two of them were lost to all time and space, oblivious to interested passersby.

"All passengers for Flight one fourteen—"

In her passion-drugged state, Alex was only dimly aware of some announcement ringing out from the speakers, but its message must have penetrated Vince's brain and jerked him back to reality. He tore his lips from hers, muttering a low curse, and pushed her away from him. Then he turned and strode away without another word.

Feeling her knees buckle, Alex grasped the cold chrome armrest of a chair nearby and lowered herself onto it. For a few dizzy moments she was dreadfully afraid she would faint. But gradually her heartbeat slowed, she felt strength flow back into her body, and with it all the pain of loneliness and rejection. Vince wanted her, needed her every bit as much as she wanted and needed him; that kiss proved it. But rather than admit the truth, he was running away. Yes, she knew now why he was leaving her, using the pretext of business. He didn't trust himself to be around her. He was afraid she might begin to pull down the bricks of that impenetrable wall he had erected between them, and to keep that from happening he would keep distance between them.

This insight into his actions, astute as it might be, offered pitifully small consolation to Alex that afternoon and during the days that followed.

Vince had promised to telephone and he did, from wherever he happened to be: New York, Los Angeles, Dallas, Seattle, and numerous other major cities in the country. Alex noted irrelevantly that all his travel now was confined to the U.S. when in the past he had traveled extensively in foreign countries as well.

In response to his inquiries about her health, she always assured him she was fine, as indeed she was. When he was satisfied on that subject, she narrated with genuine enthusiasm the progress being made on the house. For, once having resigned herself to Vince's absence, she had thrown herself unreservedly into the numerous projects necessary for completion before the house would be not just ready but perfect, as she determined it would be.

At the end of two hectic months, she deemed the house ready for occupation. For some months to come, perhaps even years, she would be on the lookout for the very special odd piece of furniture or painting or sculpture, but essentially the house was furnished and decorated and gleaming with wax and polish. It had been a monumental task to complete in so short a time, but Alex had been buoyed by an obsession to get it done. She convinced herself that Vince would have to come home now to see the finished product. When he telephoned again, she would have no compunction about using any guile or method of persuasion at her disposal to bring him back to her.

Once he saw the house, how beautiful it was, how perfect, like a finely crafted piece of jewelry, he would know she had created it lovingly for the two of them and he wouldn't be able to leave her alone for such a long time again . . . *would he*? That tiny doubt always recurred to undermine her confidence, and it was lurking beneath her breathless anticipation the evening she awaited Vince's arrival. He had refused her offer to meet him at the airport in Atlanta, saying he didn't know for sure what flight he would be taking.

She heard the car in the driveway and sped to open the door before he had a chance to ring the lovely chimes. Her premeditated plan to greet him with a kiss that would leave no doubt of the warmth of his welcome miscarried. A briefcase in one hand and a suitcase in the other, he walked past her through the open door with a polite greeting, as though he had been gone for two days rather than two months and she was his hostess rather than his wife.

Smarting under the rebuff, Alex followed him into the foyer and read the appreciation in his face as he looked around him. "I can't wait to see the rest of it," he said, sounding as if he really meant it.

The admiration was balm to her spirit, but she did wish he would look at her, as he seemed loath to do. "Wait until you see your room," she said lightly, walking past him to the stairs and intensely aware of him behind her as she ascended them, the silken folds of her long skirt grasped in one hand. For Vince's homecoming she was wearing a new hostess gown that left little of her figure to the imagination.

He didn't exclaim over the room or make effusive

compliments on its handsome masculine décor, but she could tell he liked it. She had strived to achieve an atmosphere that was soothing and restful and decidedly homey in contrast to the impersonal motel rooms he had lived in for years. From the expression in his dark eyes as he looked around, missing no detail, she knew she had succeeded. The knowledge perhaps made her reckless.

"Do you want to shower and change before dinner?" she suggested, noticing he looked tired. "There'll be plenty of time to look at the rest of the house. I hope you'll be here a while."

"Yes I would," he said in answer to the first and ignoring all the rest. He slipped off his suit jacket and hung it on the mahogany valet stand that was one of Alex's real finds after a protracted search through many antique shops. She stood her ground inside the door of his bedroom, watching with more than casual interest as he stripped off the tie and began to unbutton his shirt. His fingers halted in their task and stayed in place as he glanced around at Alex, as if just grown aware she hadn't moved. The questioning lift of his eyebrows challenged her presence, the dark eyes holding no invitation. Alex was tempted to do the cowardly thing, to turn and flee, but she reminded herself of the passionate kiss that day at the airport and its unspoken message. The memory bolstered her depleted courage.

"Do you mind if I stay and talk to you while you dress?" It wasn't easy to smile and attempt to act natural, as if her request were that of a normal wife, when the room was suddenly rife with tension and powerful undercurrents of emotion and Vince's face had gone dark with color.

"I'd rather you made me a drink."

He had turned his back to her and was peeling off the shirt. The sight of his broad shoulders and the back smoothly ridged with muscles made her hands curl involuntarily with the urge to walk up close to him and run her palms over the firm masculine flesh. The urgency of the impulse quickened her heartbeat and made her breathing shallow, as though she had run up the stairs. If only she *dared*—

"Would you like me to bring it up here?" Her husky voice was threaded with an undertone of pleading.

He stood very still, with his back to her. His hands were poised to unbutton the waistband of his beltless slacks, but he made no move to finish undressing. She could see the muscles corded along his shoulders and ridging his back; his biceps were bulging, as though he were exerting great physical power against some unmovable object. He was tensed and on guard to protect himself from unexpected attack out of the darkness.

"Thanks, no. I won't be long."

His voice told her plainly to leave him alone, to stop clawing at the wall between them. Alex turned, half blinded by hurt and rejection and frustration. *I'm not going to leave you alone, Vince!* she vowed inwardly. And she meant every word of it. No matter how low her pride sank, she refused to give up. She couldn't afford to accept defeat because her happiness depended upon breaking through Vince's defenses. She was convinced, too, that *his* happiness depended upon it. Otherwise, she might have lacked the courage to keep trying.

What she didn't know while she was rebuilding her firm resolutions in the face of his rejection was that Vince had no intention of giving her the opportunity to wear him down. He retired to his room not long after dinner with the apologetic explanation that he was dead on his feet. Alex believed him, for he looked exhausted. There was always tomorrow, she told herself.

At breakfast the next morning, he dropped the news that he was catching a plane at noon for Los Angeles. Alex just stared for several moments without speaking, disappointment twisting and knotting her insides and en-

gendering a raw new emotion she had never until that
second felt toward Vince—anger. How could she prove
to him she loved him, how could she help him to learn
to trust her if they were never together? One person
couldn't do *all* the trying—didn't he realize that?

Stung to the quick, Alex didn't attempt to persuade
him to change his travel plans and stay longer, nor did
she insist when he refused her offer to drive him to the
airport. He explained that he had a rental car parked
outside, and it would be simpler to drive that and turn
it back in himself. After he had left, she sat in the library
for hours, not moving and at first feeling nothing but
numbness. Psychologically, Vince had knocked the wind
out of her and she was trying to suck some air back into
her lungs.

For two months she had driven herself remorselessly
to get this house ready, telling herself that once it was
done, Vince would return and share it with her and everybody would live happily ever after. Her fairy tale hadn't
ended right, and deep down she was terrified that her
hopes might be just that, a fairy tale. She and Vince
might never resolve their differences. For the first time,
she permitted herself to consider that chilling possibility.

She had been so sure she could force him to respond
to her—she was still sure, but she had underestimated
him. He had side-stepped her advances with devastating
effectiveness by simply leaving again. His message was
coming through to her with ringing clarity: he wouldn't
stand for her to intrude upon his privacy. If she insisted
upon trying, he wouldn't come near her. What choice
did she have other than to leave him firmly positioned
behind his shield? None, if she wanted to see him.

Perhaps Vince was able to tell just from their telephone conversations that she had capitulated and was no
longer a menace to the emotional distance he kept between them, for after that first visit and precipitous leave-
taking he returned more frequently and stayed longer,

sometimes as long as three days. Alex was torn as to deciding which was worse, being alone in the house and longing for Vince to be there with her as her husband and lover or having him there in the role of a polite, considerate stranger. Actually, neither situation was tolerable, but what was she to do about it?

Chapter Eleven

"ALEX, PREGNANCY AGREES with you—you've never looked prettier or healthier!" Jinx proclaimed after subjecting Alex to a thorough scrutiny.

"I've never felt healthier, Jinx," Alex said truthfully, pleasure at seeing her friend blotting momentarily her aching unhappiness. "Would you like to see the house before we have lunch?"

"I'd love to. Do you know, I've admired this house ever since I can remember. I couldn't believe your good luck when I heard you and your new husband had bought it. When do I get to inspect *him*?"

With characteristic bluntness, Jinx brought out into the open the underlying cause for Alex's sense of awkwardness with this woman who had been such a good friend. Even though Alex had been married now for four months, not even her closest friends had met Vince, and she herself studiously avoided contact with them. It had taken someone with Jinx's nerve to call her up last week and insist on an invitation to lunch.

"I don't get to see him much myself," Alex evaded. "He's out of town on business most of the time." She drew her friend's attention to the beautiful old leaded-glass windows in the library, hoping to divert her from the subject of Vince. The thought of him brought Alex such pain that she would have the greatest difficulty discussing him with someone as shrewdly observant as Jinx without disclosing that all was not well in her life.

"The house is as lovely on the inside as the outside," Jinx declared when the tour was completed and she and Alex had sat down to lunch. "You've done a beautiful job furnishing and decorating it, too. I can see that money has been no obstacle." Her good-natured irony changed to slight wistfulness. "It must be nice to have a home like this."

"It is nice," Alex agreed. "It was fun getting it ready to move into—but you can't imagine how much work. I think I lived either in my car or on the telephone for two whole months!" What she didn't mention was the reason she had thrown herself heart and soul into the selection of furniture and wallpaper and draperies, the supervision of various work crews too. She had wanted to create a warm, beautiful home for Vince, a purpose that seemed ironic now since he so rarely was home to enjoy it, and when he was, he was like a privileged visitor rather than a husband. Not even to a friend like Jinx could Alex bear to reveal that she and Vince slept in separate bedrooms and that he avoided touching her in even the most casual way.

"With all this, Alex—" Jinx swept one hand in a comprehensive gesture to indicate the lovely old house, "—and the baby you've wanted so badly for years—why aren't you *happy*?"

Had Jinx spoken in her brusque lawyer manner, Alex would have stood the chance of bluffing her way through an evasive answer, but the question held such puzzled regret and the blue eyes were so filled with deep concern that Alex's defensive exterior crumbled. She hadn't fooled Jinx for one moment.

"I am happy part of the time," she said sadly. "Especially when I feel the baby inside of me and there's nobody else in the world, just him and me!" Her lips curved tenderly and her eyes took on a dreamy expression for just a fleeting moment.

"And I love this wonderful old house . . . and I love my husband . . ." Her voice grew low and strained as she struggled to control her emotion. "But, Jinx, I've hurt him too many times—I'm *afraid* . . ." Her eyes were glazed with a mist of anguish as they met those of her friend and her mouth quivered convulsively, but no tears came. Alex knew from bitter experience that they brought no relief.

"What are you afraid of, Alex?" Jinx pressed gently.

Alex bit her lips to still their trembling. Her hazel eyes were darkened with pain and fear. "I'm afraid I may have killed his love," she said gravely. Jinx was quiet, uttering none of the soothing platitudes a lesser friend might have mouthed.

Alex poured forth the whole story from the beginning, when Vince had courted her the first time. Her words came in torrents punctuated now and then by long pauses when she became immersed in her recollections. Jinx said little and her face showed almost nothing of what she thought.

The revelation had a cathartic effect on Alex. When it was over she felt like a wrung-out sponge, empty of all emotion but at the same time more at peace than she had been in months.

"Thank you," she said softly. "I guess I really needed that."

Jinx looked up from the arrangement of silk flowers in the middle of the table. "It's always a mistake to keep everything bottled up inside. Somehow it seems to get things in perspective to say them out loud to someone else." She paused and underwent a mental debate. "Imagine how Vince must feel. How many years has he been carrying this weight around? Just from what you've told me about him, he doesn't sound like the kind of man who would find it easy to talk about his private thoughts."

Alex stared at her friend. "You know, I've never thought about it like that. I've just thought he was being unreasonable not to forget the past and start all over again, fresh. Maybe he can't."

"What are you going to do, Alex?" The subtle emphasis in the question widened Alex's eyes in puzzlement.

"Do? What *can* I do? I told you; I tried." She had explained the present impasse in her relationship with Vince. If she tried to enforce intimacy, she would see even less of him than she did now.

"I can't tell you what to do. You will have to figure that out for yourself." The brisk lawyer was coming out in Jinx now. "But you won't convince me any man would take care of a woman the way Vince takes care of you if he didn't feel a great deal for her. You're not going to gain anything by acting the martyr." She glanced down at her watch. "Hey—look at the time! I'm due in court this afternoon."

Alex didn't argue when her friend ordered her to stay seated. "I'm smart enough to find my own way out of a house once I've managed to get inside," Jinx said wryly, and added with deliberate irony, "don't wait so long before inviting me again." They both laughed at this bald reminder that she had been forced to initiate the invitation herself.

"I will invite you again—soon," Alex promised warmly.

Alex lost all track of time as she sat contentedly, her eyes closed and a smile curving her lips as new hope stirred inside her, becoming somehow a part of that movement in her womb. From somewhere in the house she could hear evidence of the presence of Mrs. Whitaker, the live-in housekeeper Vince had hired over Alex's protests that she was capable of taking care of the house herself, for a while longer at least. Sometimes she suspected Mrs. Whitaker was watchdog as well as housekeeper, instructed to guard over Alex and make sure she did nothing strenuous.

Jinx was right when she said Vince took very good care of her. He was generous to a fault, giving her everything money could buy, everything in fact except the most important thing of all—himself. Was Jinx also right in suggesting Alex should try again to bridge the distance between herself and Vince? Was it true that she, Alex, had been acting the role of a martyr? After all her resolutions not to let pride take the upper hand, had she done just that?

Alex had ample time to mull over these questions since Vince did not return to Stokely until later that week. For his first evening home she planned a special dinner and wore an outfit cleverly designed to conceal the softly burgeoning evidence of her pregnancy. The floor-length gown had a scooped neckline that showed a generous view of cleavage, the skirt falling in delicate gathers from a high waistline, the fabric a soft polyester velour the color of the blush on a ripe peach.

She waited for Vince in the library, the room they both seemed to prefer over the larger and more formal living room. It was cool enough in the evenings for a fire now, and Alex was standing at one side of the fireplace gazing into the flames when Vince entered the room. She looked up and caught the unguarded expression on his face as he first saw her, and for a moment her heart leaped in response to the light in his eyes. Then a veil dropped, and he greeted her politely.

"You're looking well, Alex."

She concealed her disappointment, consoling herself

with the flame of desire she had seen flare briefly in his dark eyes before he withdrew behind his implacable wall. At least she knew he wasn't so impervious to her as he liked to appear.

"Welcome home," she said warmly and walked straight up to him and raised herself on her tiptoes to kiss him full on the mouth. Unless it was her own imagination, the strong fingers moved caressingly against the soft fabric covering her shoulders for just an instant before he removed her firmly from him.

Discouragement surged through her at his rebuff. He wasn't going to make it easy for her, but she couldn't give up. Somehow she had to penetrate that barrier with which he surrounded himself.

"Can I make you a drink?" she offered, turning back toward the fireplace. He asked for Scotch and water, and she mixed the drink from the ingredients already assembled on a tray and handed it to him.

She suspected him of having deliberately chosen the wing-backed chair rather than the sofa so that she couldn't sit beside him. Determined not to be foiled, she sank down on the rug in front of the fireplace, leaning forward and resting her weight on the palm of one hand so that the deep neckline of her gown gaped to reveal the rounded tops of her breasts, which had grown fuller with pregnancy.

"Should you sit on the floor like that?" he asked stiffly, his eyes fixed on the sensuous curves swelling from the top of her gown.

"Why not?" she countered. "With just a few exceptions—such as riding horseback, which I wouldn't do anyway—I can do everything an ordinary woman does."

His face suffused with color as he tore his eyes from her breasts and gazed down into his drink. Sensing a weakening of his armor, Alex rose to her knees in front of him, balancing her palms lightly on his thighs, which felt as rigid as steel under her touch.

"Vince, I *want* to do everything an ordinary woman does—*with her husband*!" The last words came out in a whisper.

He made a sound half curse and half groan and put his glass down on the table beside him with a dull clanking sound before reaching down and lifting her into his lap. His arms closed around her, pulling her hard up against him so that she could feel the shudder running through his body.

"You're so damned beautiful," he murmured as his hold loosened to give him access to her chest. His lips trailed a fiery path across her bared curves, eliciting a little moan of helpless pleasure from her.

She waited for what seemed eons as his fingers struggled with the zipper of her dress and finally slid it down. He gazed down at the fullness of her breasts nestled alluringly in lacy half-cups of her strapless bra, and his fingers trembled against her sensitized flesh as he pushed the bra down around her waist and cupped her breasts in his hands. He bent his head and she gasped with delight at the warm roughness of his tongue against her taut nipples and grabbed his head and hugged it to her, murmuring her pleasure.

His mouth seemed to burn whatever it grazed—her breasts, her neck, her shoulders, her lips, and every inch of her face. He seemed driven by a great hunger that had been deprived far too long, his hands urgent as they caressed and explored the intimate curves of her body, careless of the expensive fabric of her gown.

"Vince, I want you!" she whispered.

Her breathing, like his, came in great heaving gasps as he stood up with her still in his arms and carried her out of the room and up the stairs, his heart pounding against her. Desire pulsed in her veins, making her weak with anticipation of the intimacy she had dreamed of so often these last few months.

He pushed open the door of her bedroom and carried her over to the bed, laid her carefully on top of the satin

spread and then leaned over her, kissing and caressing
her face and neck and shoulders as though consumed
with a desperate hunger for the touch of her flesh. Her
heart throbbed with almost unbearable happiness that
finally they would know the oneness she so longed for—
finally she would be truly his wife.

Winding her arms around him, need having disposed
of the last shreds of her inhibitions and pushed her beyond
the bounds of patience, she urged him to hurry and pos-
sess her. When he had finally managed with unsteady
hands to push the dress down past her hips, she helped
him remove her undergarments, leaving her completely
naked to his gaze. She tugged impatiently at the fabric
of his shirt, wanting him to remove his clothes too, for
he was still fully dressed, even though she had unbuttoned the shirt and pulled it free of his trousers.

Some warning penetrated her passion-drugged euphoria, and she realized he had gone completely still and
was no longer touching her as he stared down at the
gentle swell of her abdomen. And then abruptly he moved
off the bed and stood with his back to her, shaking his
head slowly from side to side, fists clenched at his side.

"Vince, please!" she begged. "It's *all right* for us to
make love. It won't hurt the baby."

He turned around abruptly revealing the violence of
his emotion and the monumental effort he was making
to control himself. "I don't *want* to make love to you,
Alex," he grated out between clenched teeth, and she
could see his chest rising and falling with the tremendous
effort of his breathing. "Can't you understand that? I
can't stand the sight—the touch—"

She made a little hurt, whimpering sound and he
stopped abruptly, squeezing his eyes tight as if to block
out the sight of her lying there, and then wheeled and
strode out of the room. She remained in the same position
on the bed, writhing in her shame and frustration and
wishing hysterically she could just die.

Sometime later Mrs. Whitaker tapped on the door and

called to her in a concerned tone. Numbly she got up and pulled on a robe before opening the door.

The housekeeper had a tray in her hands, and Alex knew even before she was told that Vince had given instructions for her dinner to be brought up to her. He had known she wouldn't make any effort on her own to eat. A wave of bitterness swept Alex. Why should he care whether she took proper care of herself? He obviously hated her for what she had done to him.

The answer came immediately. The baby, of course. He was taking care of his child, not Alex. Somehow she found a small measure of comfort in that thought. The baby was half hers, and if Vince could love her unborn baby, perhaps one day he might be able to forgive its mother.

Alex and Vince never spoke of what had happened between them that night. He continued to travel on business, coming home infrequently. The only difference during the last weeks of her pregnancy was that he telephoned every night when he was away.

Alex resolutely concerned herself almost entirely with thoughts of the life growing inside her, and much to her surprise and gratitude, she felt very much at peace. Much of her time was taken up with shopping for the baby's things and with furnishing and decorating the nursery. All her life's energy seemed channeled into the creation of a new being and lovingly providing him with everything he would need upon arrival.

She refused to allow her mind to linger on the possibility that things might continue unchanged between herself and Vince after the baby was born. If she had, she would have been unhappy, and that would have been detrimental to the baby's welfare.

Her parents and friends marveled over her beauty every time they saw her, and it was true she had never looked lovelier, even with the increasingly ungainly bulk of her body. When Vince was home, she would look up and catch him staring at her as she sat and read or worked on some small garment she was embroidering. She would smile at him, wishing he could share this totally absorbing experience which had made a captive not just of her body but her soul as well.

Some instinct told Alex that Vince would be away when the baby was born. If their relationship had been different, she would have asked him not to go when he left on another business trip two weeks before the baby was due. Dismissing her intuitions as mere edginess resulting from the severe discomfort she was beginning to feel—no position, either sitting or lying, was comfortable for more than a minute or two—she said nothing.

The afternoon of the day following his departure, she began to have the first labor pains. A telephone call to her doctor calmed her immediately, and she sat down to wait, not mentioning anything yet to Mrs. Whitaker when she appeared to announce she had to run an errand and would return in about an hour. Dr. Rodgers had assured her there would be nothing to worry about for several hours, but since it was her first child, she could come to the hospital when the pains began coming with regularity.

Under the circumstances she was in no mood for a drop-in visitor and muttered an exclamation of impatience when the doorbell chimed. One of the last people she expected to see standing outside the front door was her father, his shoulders hunched against the piercing March wind and a hat pulled low on his forehead.

"Dad! This is a surprise. Come on in out of this nasty weather!" she urged, leading him into the library where a fire crackled cheerfully in the fireplace.

In her surprise and curiosity she momentarily forgot the labor pains, which weren't occurring with any frequency. Her father must have just left the public school where he taught chemistry and biology. What had prompted the visit? A man of habit, he usually couldn't wait to get home to the comfort of his own hearth and the cup of hot coffee Alex's mother always had waiting for him. As a part-time librarian, she arrived home earlier than he did.

Realizing suddenly the reason her father was fidgeting, she exclaimed, "Please smoke your pipe, Dad—it doesn't bother me in the least."

He promptly pulled the pipe out of an inside jacket pocket and went through the process of filling it with tobacco and tamping it carefully, his movements those of one following an exacting routine. Then he clamped the pipe between his teeth, but didn't light it. She could perceive his awkwardness.

"Now why don't you tell me why you're here," she prompted gently, and just at that moment she felt a much sharper pain than she had felt before knife through her back.

He looked relieved at her directness. "I'm just following your husband's instructions that you're not to be left alone a minute while he's away. Mrs. Whitaker and I have a schedule worked out so that she can get her shopping done in the afternoon." He smiled at her surprised exclamation and then looked thoughtful. "Guess now's as good a time as any to tell you how pleased your mother and I are at the way things worked out. When you came home right after your divorce was final and told us you had a job with Vince's travel company, I really felt over a barrel, so to speak."

"*You* knew then that Vince owned Globe Travel!" Incredulity shone in Alex's face.

"'Course I knew. Vince kept in touch with me all those years. Deep down I always suspected his main motive was to find out how you were doing." He paused, removing the pipe from his mouth and cradling it in one hand. "He's the only man on earth I'd have trusted to look after my daughter in a foreign country."

Alex was too astonished to speak. Her father had known all the time that Vince was the boss of Globe Travel who would train her in Portugal and he hadn't told her! What faith and confidence he had displayed in the man who once had been his student!

Suddenly she wondered just how much her father knew about the circumstances of her marriage to Vince and their strained relationship. She decided to approach the matter obliquely.

"I hope Vince won't travel so much after the baby is born," she said wistfully.

Her father observed her thoughtfully and nodded, as if he understood the real message beneath her words. "Vince is a man who's lived with a dream so long he's afraid to believe it's actually come true," he said quietly. "It may take some time for things to work out, but they will—if you're willing to wait."

"I have no choice, Dad," she said simply. "I love him. I just hope I haven't destroyed his love for me." She shifted uncomfortably, the ache in her back having gained an intensity that made it difficult for her to ignore it. She decided suddenly not to wait for Mrs. Whitaker to return from her shopping.

"Dad," she said casually so as not to alarm him, "would you drive me to the hospital?"

The next afternoon when Alex awoke in the hospital, the long night behind her seemed like a pain-wracked nightmare. She felt a moment of panic as her hands found her much-diminished stomach and asked anxiously of the nurse who came to stand beside the bed, "My baby—is my baby all right?"

"You have a healthy boy, honey," the woman reassured. "You had a real hard time of it, but both of you are going to be fine."

"Can I see him?" Her voice still held anxiety. She wanted to see for herself that her baby was all right.

"Why, sure you can see him," the nurse soothed.

A few minutes later, her heart swelled with love and tender pride as she examined her tiny son thoroughly, making sure he had the correct number of fingers and toes and delighting in his miniature perfection. She felt an overwhelming sense of awe, as if she had participated in a miracle.

"You know—I think you were worth it, young Mr. Vincent Reardon. I just hope your father likes you as much as I do. Maybe when he sees you, he'll like me again too, because I do love him so very, very much." She bent and pressed her lips gently against the soft fuzz covering the little head.

A movement at the door a few seconds later attracted her attention, and she looked up. Vince came slowly into the room, stopping at the end of the bed and staring at her and the baby nestled beside her. The joy his appearance aroused in her overflowed into her voice as she urged, "Come and see your son, Vince. He's beautiful!"

He didn't move. "Are you all right? The doctor said . . ." The words came out jerkily.

"I'm fine. The baby's fine—see for yourself," she assured him happily.

He came closer and leaned over to look at the infant, but went immediately to stand beside the window, his whole manner distraught as he gazed back at her. Alex felt a surge of disappointment at his failure to express any of the love and pride she felt for their son. She didn't protest when a nurse came to take the baby back to the nursery.

"Vince . . . aren't you happy you have a son?" she asked in a low, hurt tone.

He moved swiftly to the bed and then stopped abruptly, sitting down very carefully on the edge and taking her hands in both of his. Alex discovered then that he was trembling.

"At this moment I can't think of anything except—I might have . . . lost you," he said in a ragged, tormented voice, staring down at her.

"Darling, I'm fine," she assured. "Women have babies every day."

"You won't have any more," he promised tersely and bent over and kissed her lips, her cheeks, her brow, with the utmost gentleness, as if afraid she might break. "It's not worth the risk."

"But I thought children were important to you," she protested faintly, finding it difficult to concentrate on anything except this blissful closeness of her husband as he covered her face with kisses as light as feathers.

"I never even mentioned children—you did," he contradicted, bringing her palm up to his mouth and kissing it before stroking her hand against the hard plane of his cheek. For the first time since he had entered the room, she saw the ghost of a smile on his lips. "That first night in Lisbon, I was about to say the only reason to marry a woman is if you can't bear the thought of living without her, which, incredibly, was the way I felt about you at that moment—after seven long years of trying to get you out of my bloodstream."

Her heart pounded with wild hope. "You haven't . . . gotten me out of your bloodstream now— have you, Vince?" she asked with a lingering trace of uncertainty.

In answer he bent forward again, framed her face very gently in both hands and lowered his lips against hers with a deep urgency that took her breath away. "God, I'll be glad when I can touch you again," he groaned, and she realized then the terrible restraint he was under because of the fear of hurting her.

Carefully she eased herself over to the opposite side of the bed. "Lie down beside me, darling," she urged. After a moment's hesitation, he stretched out beside her, his head close to hers on the pillow and one arm circling her with tender possession. For a space of time they stayed that way without talking, too deeply content at being close together for words to be necessary.

"I love you, Vince," Alex whispered finally, reaching up one hand to trace the rugged angles of his face.

"I know." His voice was muffled as he turned his face into the softness of her neck. "I heard you talking to our son."

"Eavesdropper!" she accused, her heart pounding at the tone of his voice when he said '*our son.*' She felt as if she might burst with love for the man lying beside her.

"If you like, we can get the nurse to bring him back in, and you can listen while I tell him how I feel about his mom."

She felt the curve of his smile against the sensitive flesh of her neck and eased a little closer against his long, powerful frame. "Later. Meanwhile, why don't you just tell me," she breathed.

He tensed against her, and she could sense the turmoil inside him during a long silence. It still wasn't going to be easy for him.

"I've loved you for so long, Alex, I can't remember what it was like *not* to love you."

Alex had to brace herself not to cry out with pain as the strong fingers intertwined with hers tightened convulsively in the intensity of his emotion. The wall between them had a huge gaping hole, but she wanted to kick aside every single brick once and for all.

"If you loved me, Vince, why didn't you tell me in Portugal? Or at least after we were married?" she prodded gently. "And why did you hold me off after we were married? I tried every way I could to tell you, to show you I loved you."

He didn't answer immediately, and she feared for a panicky moment her foot had come solidly against a section of brick where the mortar still held fast. And then when he did finally begin to speak, the raw torment in his voice was almost more than she could bear. Somehow they had to get through this painful time together.

"Alex, you have no concept of the hell I went through when you turned me down flat for that no-good bastard Jameson. You broke me wide open. At first I just wanted to die . . . or kill him—I couldn't decide which. It wasn't just not having you myself, it was knowing what he was going to do to you—

"It took me a long time, years, to build up scar tissue.

The first year the only thing that kept me going was some vague determination to prove you were wrong about me . . . I *would* amount to something."

"Vince, I was so young—I didn't know what I was saying," she pleaded, awash in his anguish.

He hardly seemed to hear her. "Subconsciously, I think I was hoping I'd have another chance with you someday. I turned myself into what you said you wanted in a husband. Not that there weren't lots of personal rewards in building up Globe Travel, because there were. Eventually it became my whole life.

"Then one day out of the blue I heard your voice outside Brian's office declaring you were free. Suddenly it was all possible, the dream I had nurtured for seven long years. I was so damned scared I didn't know what to do. I picked up the phone—you know the rest."

Alex's free hand caressed his hard jawline, massaging away the tenseness in the bunched muscles. She didn't know all the rest, but she was beginning to.

"You didn't want to be vulnerable to me again," she said sadly. "That's the real reason you didn't want to make love to me, even after we were married and I belonged to you. And I refused to take no for an answer. I just couldn't understand why . . ."

"I couldn't take the risk of opening that old scar. It had taken me too many years to build up protection. In Sintra when I made love to you, I felt it start to tear—"

"That was my first time to *really* make love, Vince. Did you know that?" she interposed softly, her hand smoothing the furrow between his eyebrows.

"I knew," he said huskily, and she could detect the satisfaction in his voice. "I'd been imagining that for years, and it was everything I'd thought it would be. After that I wanted you more than I ever had and you made it so plain you didn't want anything to do with marriage."

"That was mainly self-defense," she put in. "I was feeling terribly inadequate because I thought I was barren and couldn't give you children."

"You fooled me!" To temper the harshness of his words, he brought the hand laced with his up to his lips and nuzzled it lovingly.

"When I left you in New York, I was living on the frail hope that in a few months you might have had time to get over your bitterness toward marriage. I planned to come to Stokely and make a concerted attack on your defenses. Then Brian called and told me you were marrying Jameson again—" His voice shook with the violence of his emotions, recalling for Alex those attacks of savage anger.

"You went through the same pain all over again." Alex's throat was so constricted her voice came out in a hoarse whisper. She was finally able to understand fully the behavior that had been so incomprehensible to her before. It was breaking her heart to realize the unforgivable torment she had caused him.

"I've been in a hellish limbo all these months. I couldn't trust myself to be around you for long, yet I couldn't stay away."

Some deep instinct told Alex that it wasn't all out yet, but the same source of wisdom kept her quiet as Vince waged a silent struggle with himself. When he spoke, he held wide open for her the doors of that inner sanctum which made him totally vulnerable to her.

"Alex, I'm still afraid to—to *believe*..."

She knew exactly what he was trying to articulate, and as much as it hurt her to know he still couldn't trust her completely, she was deeply thankful they were able to gain this depth of communication. She felt as if her heart had almost literally made contact with his and a new strong bond had been forged between them.

"I love you, Vince. I'm as vulnerable to you now as you are to me. During the last eight months, there have been times I just wanted to give up all hope, but I couldn't. You're the whole focus of my life. All I ask is that you don't close me out again. Give me a chance to *prove* my love."

The moment was sweetly poignant for both of them. They lay close together, the tension and anxieties draining away and the warmth of their love crowding into the empty spaces created by the evacuation. For neither of them was there any awareness of the passage of time, cocooned as they were in the oblivion of closeness.

Reality intruded in the sound of exaggerated throat-clearing. A grinning nurse stood at the foot of Alex's bed holding a blue bundle. "Make way for the other member of the family," she announced cheerfully.

Alex glanced quickly at Vince and was immediately reassured by what she saw on his face. The arrival of their tiny son was no intrusion. He was the embodiment of the bond that nothing could destroy.

Introducing a unique new concept in romance novels!
Every woman deserves a...

Second Chance at Love

You'll revel in the settings, you'll delight in the
heroines, you may even fall in love with the
magnetic men you meet in the pages of...

Second Chance at Love

Look for three new
novels of lovers lost and found coming every
month from Jove! Available now:

___ 05907-2 ALOHA YESTERDAY (#10) $1.75
    by Meredith Kingston

___ 05638-3 MOONFIRE MELODY (#11) $1.75
    by Lily Bradford

___ 06132-8 MEETING WITH THE PAST (#12) $1.75
    by Caroline Halter

Available at your local bookstore or return this form to:

 JOVE PUBLICATIONS, INC.
Dept BW, 200 Madison Avenue, New York, NY 10016

Please enclose 50¢ for postage and handling for one book, 25¢
each add'l book ($1.25 max.). No cash, CODs or stamps. Total
amount enclosed: $_____ in check or money order.

NAME_____

ADDRESS_____

CITY_____STATE/ZIP_____

Allow three weeks for delivery.   SK-20